P9-BZY-718

92   Fritz, Jean
Roo
            Bully for you,
            Teddy Roosevelt!

PLEASANT GROVE ELEM SCHOOL

Bound to Stay Bound Books, Inc.

Bully for You, Teddy Roosevelt!

Bully for You, Teddy Roosevelt!

JEAN FRITZ

Illustrations by Mike Wimmer

G. P. PUTNAM'S SONS   NEW YORK

Text copyright © 1991 by Jean Fritz
Illustrations copyright © 1991 by Mike Wimmer.
All rights reserved. This book, or parts thereof,
may not be reproduced in any form without permission
in writing from the publisher.
G. P. Putnam's Sons, a division of
The Putnam & Grosset Book Group
200 Madison Avenue, New York, NY 10016
Published simultaneously in Canada
Printed in the United States of America
Book design by Kathleen Westray
The text was set in 12 pt. Garamond
Library of Congress Cataloging-in-Publication Data
Fritz, Jean.
Bully for you, Teddy Roosevelt! / by Jean Fritz.
p.   cm.
Includes bibliographical references.
Summary: Follows the life of the dynamic twenty-sixth president,
discussing his conservation work, hunting expeditions, family life,
and political career.
1. Roosevelt, Theodore, 1858–1919—Juvenile literature.
2. Presidents—United States—Biography—Juvenile literature.
[1. Roosevelt, Theodore, 1858–1919. 2. Presidents.] I. Title.
E757.F85   1990
973.91'1'092—dc20
[B] [92] 90-8142 CIP
ISBN 0-399-21769-X

1 2 3 4 5 6 7 8 9 10

First Impression

FOR JULIE AND GREG

I am indebted to Dr. John Gable,
Executive Director of the Theodore Roosevelt Association,
for his suggestions and his help.

Bully for You, Teddy Roosevelt!

1

WHAT DID Theodore Roosevelt want to do? Everything. And all at once if possible. Plunging headlong into life, he refused to waste a single minute. Among other things, he studied birds, shot lions, roped steer, fought a war, wrote books, and discovered the source of a mystery river in South America. In addition, he became governor of New York, vice-president of the United States, then president. This was a big order for one man, but Theodore Roosevelt was not an everyday kind of man. He was so extraordinary that when people tried to describe him, they gave up on normal man-size words. "A cyclone," that's what Buffalo Bill called him. Mark Twain said he was "an earthquake." He was called "an eruption," "an express locomotive," "a buzz saw," "a dynamo."

But he did not start out this way. Indeed, he was so

puny that his parents worried if he would ever grow up at all. Born in New York City on October 27, 1858, Theodore (or Teddy, as he was called) was the second of the four Roosevelt children, and he was the sickly one, the one with asthma. As a child, he spent much of his time struggling just to get his breath. Often he would have to be propped up with pillows and would sit up in bed all night. If this didn't help, his father would pick him up and walk with him, hour after hour. Sometimes his father would bundle him up and take him out in his carriage, even though it was late at night. Then Mr. Roosevelt would drive his horses pell-mell through the city streets, careening around corners, hoping that the speed would force air into Teddy's lungs. As a last resort, Mr. Roosevelt would light a cigar and make Teddy puff on it. Inhaling the smoke was not pleasant, but it might start Teddy's lungs working again.

Not only sick, Teddy was often scared. As a little boy, he insisted that a werewolf lay at the foot of his bed, waiting to spring at him. For a while he dreaded going to church. Once he heard the preacher talking about "zeal." He didn't know what "zeal" was, but it sounded like something alive and hungry. Something that would like to eat him up. He pictured it crouching in the dark corners of the church, watching for a chance to *get* him. When he was grown up, he admitted that he had been "nervous and timid" as a child.

But he was not nervous when he was with his father. Indeed, Teddy liked nothing better. Theodore Roosevelt, Sr.—a loving and well-beloved man with a high sense of duty—was the idol of his children. Anna (or Bamie) was four years older than Teddy and considered herself one of the adults of the family, but the three younger children, Teddy, Elliott (a year and a half younger), and Corinne (three years younger), competed for their father's attention. In the morning they would stand at the foot of the stairs, waiting for their father to come down for morning prayers. As soon as he appeared, they would shout, "I speak for you and the cubbyhole too!" The cubbyhole was the space between their father and the arm of the sofa where he sat. Whoever got that seat felt special. In the evening the three would wait for their father's return, follow him to his bedroom, and watch him empty his pockets of trinkets. Some were familiar, some were new, and on lucky days some were surprises for the children. The house revolved around Mr. Roosevelt. So anxious was Teddy to please his father that later he said his father was the only man he had ever feared. Even the thought of disappointing him was more than he could bear.

Yet there was one thing about his father that Teddy could not understand nor perhaps quite forgive. He was only six in the spring of 1865 when the Civil War ended, but Teddy couldn't help hearing a great deal about it. Grown-ups talked of little else. And although Mr. Roosevelt worked hard for the Union cause, he did not fight in the war. He did not wish to upset Mrs. Roosevelt, who was from Georgia and favored the South. But Teddy had been brought up on hero stories and knew how heroes should act. How could a man not fight in a war, if there was a war right under his nose? Once Teddy was mad at his mother, and that night while saying his prayers, he let God and his mother know what *he* thought of the war. Kneeling by his bed with his mother at his side, Teddy shouted at God. Beating the Southern troops was not enough, he cried; God should "grind them to powder." (He would have been even madder at his mother if he'd known how funny she thought this was.)

Except for his sickness (and he had periods when he was all right), Teddy Roosevelt had a happy childhood. Because his father didn't think he was well enough to go to school, he had tutors come to the house to teach him. This was fine with Teddy. He had more time to read and more time to follow his "career." When he was seven years old, Teddy Roosevelt became a naturalist. It all started one morning at the market where he was sent to buy strawberries. There, laid out on a slab of wood, was a seal. Teddy knew from books what a seal was, but here was a real one that had once been alive, living its own mysterious life. Day after day Teddy went back to study that seal. With his ruler he measured its total length, the length of its tail, its head, its size around the middle. Everything that he could measure, he measured, and wrote it all down in a notebook. It was as if this information were making this wonderful wild thing *his.* In the end he did manage to take the seal's skull home, and then and there he began what he called The Roosevelt Museum of Natural History.

From that time on, there was no telling what one might find in the Roosevelt house. Some people learned to inspect the water pitcher for a snake before pouring a drink and to examine a chair for frogs before sitting down. Much to the cook's annoyance, she once found a snapping turtle tied to the leg of the sink, but when Teddy brought home a dead woodchuck and asked her to boil it, she put her foot down. Out! Out! Teddy explained that this was a scientific experiment, but the cook didn't care. Nor did Teddy's mother care when she threw out a litter of dead field mice she found in the icebox. It was a loss to science, Teddy moaned, but he wasn't discouraged. He advertised for living field mice, for which he offered to pay ten cents apiece or thirty-five cents for a family. As it happened, however, the Roosevelts, all but Bamie, left for the Berkshire Hills at about the time the advertisement appeared. And there was Bamie, left with hundreds of field mice to deal with, one way or another.

Teddy not only collected insects and animals but also observed them, and filled his notebook with his discoveries. The tree spider, he wrote, was "grey spotted with black" living in "communitys of about 20" under patches of loosened bark. The living animals—the squirrels, the guinea pigs, the mice—he named. Lordy and Rosa were two white mice he kept in separate cages, but it was Brownie, a common brown mouse who got crushed, whom Teddy mourned. Brownie was his favorite.

Summers, when they went to the country, were the best time for Teddy's explorations. All year the children looked forward to the summer, when they were free to run barefoot, to ride their Shetland pony, Pony Grant (named for Ulysses Grant, the Civil War general), to build wigwams, to play cowboys and Indians and all sorts of make-believe games that Teddy invented. As for Teddy, one of his greatest joys was to wander through the woods, identifying the birds and learning their calls. One wonderful day in 1868 he didn't need to go to the woods. The birds came to him. Seventy-five migrating swallows flew into the house, fluttering from room to room, zooming in to land on curtains, on the wall, on the floor. One landed right on Teddy's pants, which of course made him a special friend. All his life Teddy loved birds and no matter where he was or how busy, he gossiped about their coming and going as if they were neighbors. The arrival of a thrush in spring was news to be reported in a letter. The song of a chirpy sparrow was dinner-table conversation. But in May 1869, just as the children were planning their summer in the country, they were told that this year they wouldn't be going. Instead, they were all going to Europe. They would spend a year there, traveling about, seeing historic sites, visiting museums.

The children were not pleased. A whole year! Dragged from country to country with no barefoot time, no Pony Grant. It turned out just as they feared. Once they started, they kept on the go, climbing on and off trains, steamers, carriages, stagecoaches, horses, donkeys, and mules. And they walked. Teddy walked nineteen miles at one stretch, twenty at another, and climbed an 8,000-foot mountain. Before they were through, they had visited eight countries and stayed in sixty-six hotels. Although Teddy said that he "cordially hated" that year, he also had fun. Indeed, his diary shows that the younger children roughhoused whenever they could—jumping on hotel beds, having pillow fights, making war with towels, holding tickling matches when their train went through a tunnel. Once in a hotel they ganged up on a waiter and a chambermaid, throwing paper balls at them and chasing them up and down stairs. Once Elliott shut Teddy in a closet and it took their father three-quarters of an hour to get him out. Climbing Mount Vesuvius, they threw snowballs at each other; in Rome they ran around scaring stray dogs with their cap guns.

And Teddy saw sights that impressed him: some rare black Australian swans, the Prince of Wales, two boars and a wildcat fighting in a zoo, a tree that was over fourteen hundred years old, and a gold chain that was supposed to ward off the evil eye. (He bought the chain.) When crossing from one country to another, he made a point of standing with one leg in one country and the other leg in the other. When he had one leg in France and one in Switzerland, he reported it. Also when he straddled Italy and Switzerland. All the time, however, what he really wanted was to get both legs back in America. On May 25, 1870, he finally made it. At the first glimpse of New York, he exploded with joy. "New York!!!" he wrote. "Hip, Hurrah!"

As usual, Teddy had been sick during the trip, but he was used to this so he didn't talk much about it. All over Europe Mr. Roosevelt watched Teddy gasping for breath, and although he took him to doctors, they couldn't cure him. Of course Mr. Roosevelt was pleased at how well Teddy managed between bouts, but still he worried. He believed in an active life. "Man was not intended to be an oyster," he said, and he didn't want Teddy turning into an invalid. Shortly after their return home, he called Teddy aside.

"Theodore," his father said, "you have the mind but you have not the body, and without the help of the body, the mind cannot go as far as it should. You must *make* your body. It is hard . . . but I know you will do it."

Teddy had a way of throwing back his head when he was determined, tightening his jaw, and clamping down on his words as if he meant to force them to obey him. "I'll make my body," he promised, clamping down hard.

Mr. Roosevelt made the second-floor porch into a gymnasium with weights to lift, rings to pull, horizontal bars to cross. Hour after hour, Teddy lifted, pulled, and pushed. Of course it was drudgery, but in time Teddy came to relish the very hardness of it. He liked knowing his muscles were straining to do their best work. He enjoyed pushing his body as far as it would go. He delighted in feeling every part of himself come to life.

Slowly he did grow stronger, but he was not as tough as he thought. Once, after a bad asthma attack, his father sent him for a change of air to friends in Maine. Teddy traveled alone by stagecoach with two boys about his age who were strangers to him. He had never had much contact with other children except for those in his own family, cousins, and children of his parents' friends, so he didn't know what to do about boys who were unfriendly. But when these two boys started to make fun of him, Teddy decided that this was a time to fight. It never oc-

curred to him that he couldn't do what he wanted to do, but he couldn't. Teddy was embarrassed at how easily the boys overcame him. Indeed, without even hurting him, the boys showed Teddy that he didn't know the first thing about fighting. When he returned home, Teddy asked his father for boxing lessons. Now, in addition to lifting, pulling, and pushing, he began punching.

A young teenager now, Teddy was not only making his body, he was also shaping his life. At about this time three other important things happened to him.

1. His father took him to a taxidermist's shop, where Teddy learned how to skin, stuff, and mount animals, including birds.

2. His father gave him his first gun. Teddy was fourteen and the family was spending the summer in Dobbs Ferry, New York. Teddy took his gun into the woods and began shooting birds. He loved birds as much as ever, but now that he had learned to skin and mount them, he could practice science seriously. He could also *own* some of the wildness of nature, just as he had once longed to own that dead seal.

3. He acquired his first pair of glasses. When he discovered that it was hard to see the birds he was shooting at, his father had his eyes tested. His glasses changed everything. "I had no idea how beautiful the world was," he said, "until I got those spectacles."

Teddy Roosevelt never did anything halfway. Now that he was into skinning and stuffing, he couldn't skin and stuff enough. When the family went to Europe again that fall, Teddy didn't object. He'd take his gun and all his skinning and stuffing equipment. They were going to Egypt this time, to live on a houseboat. Egypt! Just imagine the birds! From his books he knew that there would be exotic new ones, and indeed they were there waiting for him—so many and so glorious, it was as if he'd walked in on the very Creation of birds. Sardinian warblers, storks, ibises, egrets, kestrels, bulbuls, hoopoes, cranes, dunlins, and among his favorites, ziczacs who had such a crazy scream. Enraptured, Teddy went about, his head back, his eyes fixed on the sky. Still, he wasn't just admiring, he was noticing and making notes, using scientific terms to describe what the birds looked like, what their habits were, what songs they sang. (He decided that the vulture spotted its prey by seeing it, not smelling it.) When Teddy wasn't writing, he was on donkey back with his father, shooting. At the boat, he would skin and clean and stuff, but all the time he was learning, finding out what the bird ate, its coloration, the shape and size of its bill, the length of its legs. A scientist killed, he would say later, so he could create before his eyes "the life that was," not just list pieces of "the death that is."

Teddy's days were so full, so splendid, he didn't care how grubby he looked or how disgusting he smelled. Elliott, who shared a room with him, complained that not only Teddy but their room smelled of chemicals and the insides of dead birds. Corinne said she was sick and tired of the whole bird business, but Teddy went right on. At the end of their trip, he had between one hundred and two hundred specimens, many neatly mounted, each with its Latin name written in pink ink on a museum card.

Back in New York, the Roosevelts moved into a new house and Teddy was given the attic for his Museum of Natural History.

Teddy's family all supposed that when he finished college he would become a naturalist. Teddy supposed so too, but first he had to get into college. He had two years to get ready—from November 1873, when he returned from Europe, to the summer of 1875, when he would take his examinations for entering Harvard in the fall of 1876. Teddy had always been a fervent reader, never without a book to settle down with or pick up in a spare minute. He even read standing up. The other children laughed at the way he'd stand on one foot and read, the other foot raised, like a stork. But now that Teddy had a new tutor and a goal to meet, he seemed not just to read books but to devour them, gulping them down as fast as he could, one after another. Even at the Roosevelts' new summer home at Oyster Bay, Long Island, he put in long hours studying and long hours building up his body. Some might call the schedule he kept hard work. Not Teddy. Being busy was fun.

In July 1875, he took his college entrance examinations in eight subjects and passed them all. "Is it not splendid!" he wrote. (He might have said it was "bully." Anything especially splendid he liked to call "bully.") When he arrived at Harvard the next fall, he was seventeen years old, 5 feet, 8 inches tall, and he weighed 124 pounds. Actually, he had measured himself as thoroughly as if he were one of his own scientific specimens. Chest, 34 inches; waist 26½; thigh, 20; calf, 12½; neck, 14½;

shoulders, 41. He could run a hundred-yard dash in 12.25 seconds, broad-jump 13 feet, and pole-vault 5 feet, 8½ inches. Obviously, he was not a big fellow nor was he puny; still, his classmates did not know what to make of him. At first glance all anyone noticed were Teddy's glasses, which seemed too big for his face, and his teeth, which seemed too large for his mouth. And he was always in a hurry. He didn't walk if he could run. And talk! His words tumbled out so fast they tripped over each other, and once started they didn't seem to know how to stop. In one class he talked so much that the professor had to remind him who was in charge of the class. Having studied only with tutors, Teddy had never been in a class with others before, so if Harvard had to get used to Teddy Roosevelt, he also had to get used to Harvard.

And they did get used to each other. Teddy was too happy and enthusiastic a person not to make friends, and he soon felt at home in college life. What was more, although he had occasional attacks of asthma, his health was better than it had ever been. Only one thing disappointed him. His science courses. They weren't what he expected. So much laboratory work, so much looking through a microscope! Although Teddy enjoyed measuring and observing, science at Harvard seemed unconnected to the world of outdoors. To make up for this, Teddy took trips to the woods and brought back his own specimens. The summer after his freshman year, he and a college friend went to the Adirondack Mountains to catalogue the birds there. Teddy had started his own observations several years before, but now he and his friend completed the work together and published a book, *The Summer Birds of the Adirondacks.* Ninety-seven different varieties (some rare, almost unknown in the area) were listed along with a description of each.

All went well for Teddy, but anyone looking at his college career would see that it had to be cut into two parts—Before and After. The date that divided one part from the other was February 9, 1877. On that day Teddy's father died of cancer. "I felt as if I had been stunned," Teddy wrote, "or as if part of my life had been taken away. . . . He was everything to me." In his distress, Teddy may have felt that with his father's death his boyhood was gone. If so, he would have been wrong. Teddy Roosevelt would always be a boy. And living or dead, his father would always be looking over his shoulder. Teddy no more wanted to disappoint his father now than he ever had.

2

TEDDY READ something in a book once that helped him when he was afraid. If you act as if you're not afraid, the book said, you will stop feeling afraid. Why wouldn't the same idea work with unhappiness? If a person acted happy, perhaps he'd begin to feel happy again. For Teddy, being happy meant being on the go, doing things, following his many interests, using up his energy. The summer after his father died, Teddy drove himself harder at Oyster Bay than he ever had—swimming, hiking, boxing, galloping across country on his horse, Lightfoot (not too far or fast for Teddy but sometimes almost too much for Lightfoot). When he and Elliott went out on the water, he let Elliott take the sailboat. Teddy didn't like just leaning back and letting the wind push him along. He wanted to go under his own strength, so he took the rowboat. He loved feeling the power in his arms and watching the oars at work.

By the time he entered his junior year at Harvard, Teddy had partially recovered from his grief, but still in a "driving" mood, he went all-out for college activities. He joined the rifle club, the art club, the glee club, the finance club, worked on the college magazine, was elected vice-president of the Natural History Society, and was invited to join the college's most distinguished social club. In addition, he took nine courses and did well in all of them.

And he fell in love. Being Teddy, he didn't fall a little in love; he fell head over heels. Her name was Alice Lee. She was seventeen years old when Teddy met her, and according to him, she was perfect—"sweet," "enchanting," "bright," "endearing," "a rare and radiant maiden." But she was not easy to win. Indeed, she may have found Teddy hard to get used to, so he made sure she saw him a lot. He had Lightfoot shipped up to Harvard in the spring, and the poor horse was kept busy, rain or shine, galloping the six miles back and forth to Chestnut Hill, the Boston suburb where Alice lived. On days when Alice seemed to encourage him, Teddy's happiness gushed up in his diary like a geyser gone wild. *Alice, Alice, Alice,* her name was all over the pages—and then one day her name disappeared. All we read about now is that Teddy couldn't sleep. One night he didn't even go to bed. Also, he was starting to write a book about the War of 1812. As usual, he wasn't talking about his troubles; he was simply keeping busy.

Much later Teddy admitted that when he first proposed to Alice she turned him down and he went "nearly crazy." But on January 12, 1880, he reported that Alice Lee had changed her mind. She would marry him. They announced their engagement on February 14 and planned to be married on Teddy's twenty-second birthday, October 27.

Meanwhile Teddy had to decide what he would do after he had finished at Harvard. By the time he graduated, on June 30, 1880, he had given up the idea of becoming a naturalist. If Teddy wanted a scientific career, he would have to go abroad for three years of study. But he was getting married. He didn't want to hang around, waiting three more years for life to begin. He would go to Columbia University's law school. He wasn't dead sure that he wanted to be a lawyer, but lawyers often became politicians and Teddy did like to run things. Besides, Teddy would be with Alice in New York, which was where things happened.

Everything went as planned. When it came time for Teddy to say "I do," he threw back his head as he said it, and clamped his teeth down hard. No one knew that not too long before, he had said "I won't" in just that determined a way. He didn't tell Alice or his family or his diary that his doctor had told him he had a bad heart, weakened by years of asthma. The doctor told Teddy that he should plan on a quiet life in which he'd be sitting down as much as possible. This meant that he shouldn't play tennis, hike, box, swim, or ride. He should even avoid running up stairs. What the doctor described sounded exactly like the life of an oyster. Teddy told the doctor that he wasn't going to follow a single one of those instructions. He had been making his body himself for years and he would go on making it. He promised himself that he would live full-tilt until he was sixty years old and then whatever happened would be all right. Sixty seemed a long time away.

Geared as he was to a vigorous, whirling kind of life, Teddy Roosevelt probably couldn't have obeyed his doctor's orders even if he'd wanted to. Indeed, settled in New York with Alice and going to law school, Teddy soon became restless. The law in his textbooks had less to do with justice than he thought it should. He wanted to get into the "governing class," where he could go to work establishing justice in a practical way. Why not get into politics at the lowest level and see how it worked? he asked himself. But Teddy was a "gentleman," which in those days meant that he came from a long-standing aristocratic family. And high-class gentlemen did not mix with common politicians. Like Teddy's father, a gentleman worked hard on the sidelines of government, supporting good causes. Sometimes he might be invited to take a political role, perhaps be nominated as a senator, but all in a dignified way.

So far Teddy had behaved as a gentleman. He was working on the book he had started at Harvard (*The Naval War of 1812*); he was studying law; he was going to the opera and to balls. Still, he was impatient. So he began dropping in at his district's Republican headquarters—a bare, seedy-looking room above a saloon. Teddy, often appearing in evening dress on his way to the opera, must have been a shock to the local politicians—small-time landlords, saloonkeepers, horse-car conductors—who had not much use for "gentlemen." Teddy, however, decided that whether it was gentlemanly or not, he wanted to win over this group of rough, tobacco-chewing men whose English was anything but pure. Although his family told him his behavior was decidedly un-gentlemanly, Teddy continued his visits. "I went around there often enough," he said, "to have the men get accustomed to me and to have me get accustomed to them, so that we began to speak the same language." By the spring of 1881 he did feel that they were speaking the same language. More or less.

Then, on May 2, 1881, with law school over for the summer, Teddy and Alice left for Europe on their long-delayed honeymoon. "Hurrah!" he wrote, "for a summer abroad with the darling little wife." (Generally he spoke of Alice as his "little wife" or his "little pink wife," just as he referred to his mother as his "little mother.") After a month in Ireland, Teddy and Alice went on to London, Paris, Venice, and the Alps. In his free time Teddy worked on his book, and whenever he saw a mountain, he climbed it. Even the Matterhorn. Almost fifteen thousand feet high, the Matterhorn had been conquered less than twenty years before and was still luring so many men to death that it was considered the ultimate challenge. Of course Teddy had to try it. Accompanied by two guides and with the help of a forty-foot rope, he did get up and he did get down again. "It was like going up and down enormous stairs on your hands and knees for nine hours," he said.

As soon as Teddy and Alice returned to New York in the fall, Teddy went back to studying, partying, and writing. (He finished his book in December.) And when he began visiting his political friends, he discovered that they had become more used to him even than he had supposed. One of the most influential men in the group decided that Teddy would have a good chance to be elected as an assemblyman to the state legislature in Albany. So he was nominated and he was not only elected, he won with almost twice as many votes as his opponent. Teddy Roosevelt, the youngest assemblyman in New York, was in "the governing class." And there was no need, he decided, to finish law school.

Although Teddy knew he was perceived as "different," he never tried to make himself over to fit anyone's pattern. So he must have known that on his first appearance in the Assembly he would cause a sensation. Perhaps he even enjoyed it. Instead of regular glasses, he wore a pair of fancy pince-nez on his nose. His formal jacket was cut away in the front to display his vest with a gold watch chain stretched across it. The tails of his jacket reached down almost to his shoes, and his bell-bottomed trousers were so tight he looked as if he'd been poured into them. In one hand Teddy carried a gold-knobbed cane; in the other he carried his high silk hat.

The men in the room stared in disbelief and whispered. "Who's the dude?" they asked each other. Later, when Teddy began to talk, the men found him hilarious. His voice was squeaky, as if after years of asthma his vocal cords needed oiling. Moreover, he spoke with a high-society Harvard drawl. "Mis-tah Speak-ah!" he would say.

The assemblymen had all kinds of names for Teddy. "Young Squirt," they called him, "His Lordship," "Jane Dandy," "the exquisite Mr. Roosevelt." Eventually Teddy would make friends with some of these men but at the moment he considered them a "stupid, sodden, vicious lot." Still, he put up with them until one cold day in a tavern when an assemblyman, noticing that Teddy wore only a short pea jacket, walked up to him. "Won't Mamma's boy catch cold?" he sneered. At least, this was the general drift of his words. It was too much for Teddy. He took off his glasses, stood up, and knocked the man down. Not once but three times. Then he said, "Now you go over there and wash yourself."

Things went better after this and as Teddy Roosevelt picked up speed on the floor of the Assembly, it was obvious that he was made for political life. He loved nothing better than a contest and a chance to right wrongs. Perhaps he was really a preacher at heart, as some suggested. If so, he had undoubtedly picked up his strain of righteousness from his father, who not only talked about right and wrong but did something about it. Teddy, however, wanted to change everything at once. He proposed all kinds of legislation, from cleaning up New York City's water supply to cleaning up its election system.

As it turned out, Teddy was elected for three terms to the Assembly and it is no wonder that he earned himself the title "The Young Reformer." Still, even his friends ad-

mitted that sometimes he went too far. Once he actually called for a return of the whipping post for any man who inflicted pain on a "female or male under fourteen years of age." Although he knew he had a reputation for cocksureness, nevertheless Teddy said he learned something in Albany. He learned that politics is a matter of give-and-take. And he found out that he didn't know everything.

Sometimes during these years Teddy commuted to New York City to see Alice. Sometimes Alice joined him in his rooms in Albany, but their best times together came in their summers at Oyster Bay where Teddy swung into his usual vigorous routine. (Once he played ninety-one games of tennis in one day.) He was also planning to build his own home at Oyster Bay. There were five important features that the new house absolutely must have, he said: (1) It should be big enough to accommodate a big family. (2) It should have a large front porch facing the water so Teddy could sit in his rocking chair and watch the sun set. (3) It should have plenty of room for books. (4) It should have a gun room on the top floor. (5) It should have big fireplaces.

He might have come along further with his plans if he had not taken sick in the summer of 1883 between his second and third terms in the legislature. Indeed, he was so sick from a combination of asthma and an intestinal disease that his doctor ordered him to go with Alice to a health spa in the Catskill Mountains that was famous for its sulphur springs. Teddy was sick enough this time to obey his doctor's orders. But he regretted it. He had no use for the "idiot medical man" in charge of him at the spa and he hated the sulphur water he had to drink. It tasted, he wrote Bamie, as if a box of sulphur matches had been steeped in dishwater and served from an old kerosene oil can. "I am bored out of my life," he said.

Still, he did get better and this was important since he had big plans for the fall. What he needed instead of a health spa was an adventure, and he was going to the right place to find it. He had dreamed about the West ever since he'd been a boy, and now, he figured, he'd better get there while the West was still wild and before all the buffalo were gone. A friend had recommended Dakota country as a good hunting ground for buffalo, and in September Teddy said good-bye to Alice, took his guns, and hurrah! he was off.

As soon as he stepped off the train after five days of travel, Teddy could see that the West was still wild. The town at the station stop had a few ramshackle buildings and a number of equally ramshackle-looking men. It was almost as if the people felt no-account, perched as they were in the middle of nowhere. And of course it was into that "nowhere" that Teddy wished to go. So he hired a guide, twenty-five-year-old Joe Ferris, who after much persuasion agreed to take him buffalo hunting. Perhaps Joe thought that this eastern greenhorn with the big glasses would give up quickly when he discovered how hard it was to find buffalo. Just the week before, a band of Sioux Indians had killed off a herd of 10,000, and every day they were becoming more scarce.

But Joe Ferris did not know Teddy Roosevelt. Teddy fell in love with the land immediately. Known as the Bad

Lands, the country with its multicolored, strange-shaped buttes was so weird and so beautiful it looked as if it had been meant for another planet. And it was big. From the top of a butte the world ran around in a complete circle, gloriously empty of any hint of mankind. And the sky! It seemed to have dropped down just to get a closer look at Earth. How could a man like Teddy Roosevelt not respond to such a place? This was "hero country," he wrote Bamie, and indeed, being here made him feel that he could be a hero or anything else he cared to be.

Yet it was not easy country. The first day Teddy and Joe had to ford the Little Missouri River twenty-one times, go through or around bogs and quicksand, scramble up dangerously steep and slippery riverbanks. They rode forty-five miles and Joe Ferris was tired out. Not Teddy. That night at the hunting lodge he was so full of talk he didn't even want to go to bed.

The next day it rained. Knowing that the ground would turn into molasses-like mud, Joe tried to persuade Teddy to put off hunting until the weather cleared. Teddy said no. He'd come for buffalo and rain wouldn't stop him.

The third day it rained. Still Teddy insisted on going out. And the fourth day. And the fifth. On the sixth day the sun finally appeared and so did a lone buffalo, an old but lively one who took one look at the hunters and hightailed it out of sight. The men tried following his trail, but without luck.

Now that he'd actually seen a buffalo, Teddy was more determined than ever. Late in the afternoon that same day they had a second chance. This time there were three buffalo and fortunately they were far enough away so that Teddy and Joe could approach more carefully. They got off their horses, threw themselves onto the ground, and crept forward on their hands and knees. Teddy's eyes were so intent on the buffalo that he didn't see the bed of cactus until he was in it and his hands were covered with cactus prickles. He went on. He didn't stop until he was within three hundred and fifty yards of the buffalo. Then, prickles and all, Teddy aimed his rifle at the nearest animal and pulled the trigger. It was a poor aim, for although the bullet hit, it did not keep the wounded buffalo and the other two from galloping off, leaving Teddy and Joe to scramble for their horses.

Again they followed. Even after dark they followed, in the light from a full moon. This time they managed to get within twenty feet of the wounded animal, and still on horseback, Teddy fired. And he missed. Before he could fire again, the buffalo turned and charged. Teddy's horse was so frightened, he reared back his head and hit the raised rifle, slamming it against Teddy's head and sending blood pouring into his eyes. Joe fired twice, missed both times, and again the buffalo got away.

After a long day in the saddle with only a mouthful of water to drink and one hard biscuit to eat, the two men lay down that night in the open, wrapped in blankets. Then, as if they hadn't had enough bad luck, it started to rain again. By morning their blankets were soaked and they were lying in four inches of water. Joe must have thought that now they would give up; surely this would be enough even for Teddy Roosevelt. But when he looked over, Teddy was grinning. "By Godfrey, but this is fun!" he said.

Still, it was not getting a buffalo. There would be more days of drenching rain and days of blistering sun before the day would come that Teddy was waiting for. His horse alerted him. Holding up his nose, the horse sniffed the air. Teddy dismounted, hoping that the horse was smelling what he wanted him to be smelling. Walking beside his horse, he climbed a hill and looked over the top. And there below was his buffalo. "I put the bullet in his shoulder," Teddy wrote later; and although the buffalo ran off, Teddy knew he could not survive that shot. Teddy followed, and found the buffalo almost immediately "stark dead."

Teddy had been happy on all the unsuccessful days, but now with success he went wild. He pranced around the carcass of his buffalo, whooping and yelling as if he were a boy again, playing Indian. When he recovered from his caper, he reached into his pocket, pulled out a $100 bill, and gave it to Joe Ferris.

Of course Teddy was pleased that he would have his own buffalo head in New York, perhaps mounted someday on a wall in a home of his own in Oyster Bay. Still, he wasn't through with the West. The country had claimed him and he wanted a stake in it. He didn't mean to buy land but, from all he'd heard, it might be smart to buy cattle. People here were talking about what great cattle country this was, now that the Indians had given up their rights to it and now that a railroad was handy for shipping beef back East. Teddy had seen for himself the great meadows of thick green grass that grew wherever stones and sagebrush gave way. He may even have read a book telling how to get rich on the Plains. The author said that next to Montana, Dakota had some of the best grazing lands in the country. So why shouldn't Teddy invest in it? Although he received $8,000 a year from his father's estate and $1,200 as an assemblyman, it never seemed enough. And now not only would there be a new house at Oyster Bay to plan for, there would be a new member of the family. Alice was expecting a baby, due in February of the next year.

So Teddy made a profit-sharing deal with Joe Ferris's brother, Sylvane, at the Maltese Cross Ranch. He gave Sylvane $1,200 for the purchase and management of four hundred head of cattle. He would come back from time to time. After all, he had business here now.

3

A FRIEND ONCE said of Teddy: "He would go at a thing as if the world was coming to an end." Back in New York, Teddy sought his reelection to the Assembly in just this do-or-die way, and once he was elected, he threw himself headlong into his reform program. In New York City he began an investigation into the city's corruption. Then, on February 11, he returned to Albany, even though Alice's baby was due soon. But he wasn't worried about leaving. He'd be back home, he said, by February 14, about the time the baby was expected. Besides, Alice was with Teddy's mother and Bamie. Elliott lived only a block away, so everything would be under control even if the baby arrived before Teddy did.

Early on the morning of February 13, Teddy received a telegram with the news that a baby girl had been born the night before. Alice was doing "fairly well." Of course he was overjoyed, and since Alice seemed to be all right, he decided to finish up the work he'd planned for the day before going home. But several hours later another telegram arrived. Anyone who watched Teddy read that telegram knew something was terribly wrong. He didn't say what it was. He simply took the next train home.

Perhaps Teddy himself didn't know how bad the news was until Elliott met him at the front door. "There is a curse on this house," Elliott said. Their mother lay in bed on one floor, dying of typhoid fever. Alice was on another floor, dying of a kidney disease. The baby, little Alice, was fine, but Teddy had no time now to think of her. For the rest of the night he sat, cradling Alice in his arms, telling her to live, begging her to live, trying somehow to fight her battle for her. At three in the morning on February 14, Teddy's mother died. In the early afternoon Alice died.

Teddy was numb. He went through the motions of saying what he had to say, doing what he had to do, but what he wanted was to run away, to forget. He must have longed for Dakota country now, but the image of his father kept returning to him. The important thing, he told himself, was to live in such a way that would have made his father proud.

So three days later, having left the baby in Bamie's care, Teddy was back in Albany, tight-lipped and steely. At the core of his character was an iron will forged by years of intense work and determination to *make* his body. Now it forced him to work at such a pace that he looked as if he were running. And he was. He believed that anything painful in the past should be left in the past, and of course he had to run to keep ahead of the pain. After the first stages of grief, Teddy never mentioned Alice's name again. He put away her pictures and her letters, and years later, when he wrote his autobiography, he never mentioned that once there had been an Alice Lee in his life. Furthermore, he never told young Alice anything about her mother. Not once.

The entire time in Albany after Alice's death was like a nightmare to Teddy. He never wanted to see the place again, he said, let alone work in the Assembly. This sounded as if he meant to quit politics, but instead he seemed to be looking for a larger stage. In any case, he was elected a delegate-at-large to the Republican National Convention to be held in Chicago in June. He knew that a politician's future depended on how well he performed and how many friends he made in his party. Certainly Teddy Roosevelt became a conspicuous figure in Chicago. He worked tirelessly, talked endlessly, and fought stubbornly for the candidate of his choice for the Republican ticket. But his candidate lost. The Republicans nominated James G. Blaine, a man Teddy Roosevelt thoroughly disapproved of, for president.

Exhausted and cross, Teddy left the convention for Dakota country. Perhaps he was through with politics. He acted that way. As if he were turning his back on the East, he bought a broad sombrero, a fringed and beaded buckskin shirt, an alligator belt, horsehide riding trousers, cowboy boots, a braided bridle, and silver spurs. He also bought a "pearly hilted revolver" and a "beautiful finished Winchester rifle." Only one thing about him made him seem less than a genuine cowboy: his glasses. To a westerner, a man who wore glasses did not seem very manly. Cowboys, always taken aback when they first met him, often called him "Four Eyes" or "Storm Windows" behind his back. If they called him either of those names to his face, they did so only once. Teddy told one man who called him Four Eyes to to "put up or shut up." (The man shut up.) But Teddy knocked down another man who didn't have the sense to shut up.

The people in Dakota country soon learned that young Theodore Roosevelt intended to take their country seriously. That summer he purchased 1,000 head of cattle, and a few months later 1,500 more; and in short order he selected a site for a ranch of his own and hired two old friends, hunting guides from Maine, to be his foremen. The Elkhorn Ranch, he called it. Once completed, his house was the finest in the Bad Lands. It had eight rooms, a basement, a front porch facing the Little Missouri River, and a rocking chair on the front porch. Teddy couldn't get along without a rocking chair. Even when he sat down to rest, he liked to feel that at least his chair was on the go. Finally, of course, there were trophies from his hunting expeditions. Antlers of elk, like the skeletons of huge birds, flew from the rafters, perched on the porch railing, clung to the walls.

Teddy went hunting regularly, sometimes for a month or two at a time, sometimes as far away as the Bighorn Mountains. Eventually every specimen that this country offered, Teddy shot: duck, grouse, prairie chicken, dove, rabbit, bighorn sheep, elk, antelope, and—to his delight—grizzly bear. He had been impressed several years before when Elliott had gone to India and shot a tiger; so when he brought down his first grizzly, he boasted to his family. His grizzly, he reported, stood nine feet tall, weighed 1,200 pounds, and was surely just as fierce as, if not fiercer than, Elliott's tiger.

When Teddy wasn't hunting, he was writing. Again and again he expressed the wish that he would "amount to something." So if he couldn't be a politician, maybe he would be a writer. The first of his books on the West, *Hunting Trips of a Ranchman,* must have been a joy to write. Not only did he pour out his love for the West, he created an adventure story in which he was the hero. In a way it is a strange book, for although it is a record of his many kills, it is also a song of praise for all the wild creatures he loved. To Theodore Roosevelt, this was not strange. He was doing what he had always done—getting close to nature but collecting specimens to keep as his own. While exploring the wilderness, he was testing himself physically and coming back with something to show for it.

But most important, the West gave Teddy friends. Since he was a rancher, not a cowboy, he was called "Mr. Roosevelt," but he was no longer an outsider. At roundup times he was treated as an equal, working just as hard, sleeping just as little as any cowboy. Indeed, the twice-a-year roundups were an ordeal for all of them. Some 4,000 cattle, which had been wandering freely for months, had to be found, herded, and driven to central points where they could be separated according to their brands. In the spring calves had to be roped and branded. Although Teddy had practiced roping, he wasn't considered skillful enough to do it at a roundup, but after the animals had been roped, he wrestled them to the ground, helped drag them to the fire, and held them while they were branded. Like everyone else, he rode more than a thousand miles in five weeks; sometimes he rode as much as a hundred miles in one day and then took his turn as night guard. And when it came to bronco-busting, Teddy held on as well as anyone. He wouldn't give up on a bronco even when he was thrown. Once he fell backward and his shoulder was broken, but he climbed back up and went on with the roundup until it was over. "He's sure a man to hold up his end," one cowboy said of him. As for Teddy, he said his cowboy friends were "as hard and self-reliant as any men who ever breathed."

If the need arose, those cowboys would follow Mr. Roosevelt anywhere, and he knew it. When it looked as if the United States might go to war with Mexico over a border dispute, Teddy wrote to the secretary of war, offering to raise a regiment of cowboys to fight with him. They would be, he said, "as utterly reckless a set of desperadoes as ever sat in the saddle." That war never happened; this may have disappointed Teddy. Perhaps in the back of his mind, it still bothered him that his father had had the chance to be a hero in the Civil War and hadn't taken it. Teddy had always wanted the chance, now more than ever. Suppose he never amounted to anything?

Devoted as he was to Dakota country, Teddy had one foot firmly planted in the East during his entire career as a rancher. Two weeks after Alice's death, he had arranged for the construction of his house at Oyster Bay. Bamie, in addition to taking care of baby Alice, had agreed to supervise the building, but in any case Teddy would be back often. He thought nothing of rushing back and forth across half a continent. Indeed, he was hardly settled in the West before he was dashing to the East to prove to everyone that, no matter what, he was loyal to the Republican Party. Even a poor Republican, he believed, was better than a Democrat, so he supported James Blaine in the election against Grover Cleveland, the Democratic opponent. Again Teddy was on the losing side, and back West he went.

But in the summer of 1885 Teddy came East and stayed for eight weeks. The house at Oyster Bay was finished and Teddy moved in. He called the place Sagamore Hill in honor of an Indian chief who once held war councils at the site. With its twenty-three rooms, the house looked large enough to accommodate an Indian chief and his warriors, and they would have felt at home. The downstairs was a hunter's paradise, its walls crowded with the heads of animals Teddy had shot.

On the porch was a rocking chair, and Teddy would have sat in it, rocking at sunset just as he'd planned. But even when little Alice was with him, even when relatives and friends were there, he must have felt lonely. Those twenty-three rooms had been meant for a large family. And by this time he had meant to amount to something.

On August 22, 1885, Teddy returned to the Elkhorn Ranch, restless and out of sorts. In October he was back in New York, a loyal Republican ready to work for Republican candidates in the state election. Perhaps he planned a short stay, but something happened to make him change his mind. One evening as he walked through the front doorway at Bamie's house, he found himself suddenly face to face with Edith Carow coming down the stairs. Edith had grown up with the Roosevelt children, had been a frequent visitor at Oyster Bay, and at one time she and Teddy were said to be "sweet" on each other. Still, he didn't want to see her. He had specifically told Bamie to make sure that Edith was never there when he was. And now here she was, a strikingly handsome young woman whom he had deliberately avoided since Alice's death. Perhaps Teddy was afraid he might be sweet on her again and he didn't want to be. He didn't want to be sweet on anyone, for much as he wanted to forget Alice, he also wanted to be true to her.

But it was too late. He must have known immediately that he wanted to see Edith again, and he did see her. Sometimes he took her to social events; sometimes he saw her privately, for both of them knew it would be improper if a man was seen courting a woman when his wife had been dead less than two years. Nevertheless, on November 17 Edith and Teddy became secretly engaged. Edith was twenty-four years old; Teddy was twenty-seven, a robust, tan-faced young man glowing with the health he'd won in the West. They agreed to wait a year before being married, and in the meantime Teddy went to the

Elkhorn Ranch and Edith went to London with her mother and sister. When the year was up, Teddy would go to London where they would be married. Until then they would keep everything secret.

Teddy took up ranch life with his usual vigor, and when he wasn't ranching or hunting, he was writing. He had to write, he figured, as fast and furiously as he could, for as Bamie kept reminding him, he had spent too much money—$45,000 for Sagamore Hill, $85,000 for his cattle business. His books and his cattle would have to support him. He would forget about politics; that was all in the past. Yet when he delivered a Fourth of July speech at a Dakota celebration, Teddy found himself swinging into patriotic oratory that must have stirred his political ambitions. "Like all Americans," he cried, "I like big things; big prairies, big forests, big mountains, big wheatfields." As he talked, he seemed to see America stretching ever bigger and bigger. There was no end to what America could be. Nor to what he could be. Or so his voice implied.

The audience roared its approval. The editor of a newspaper was so impressed he asked Teddy what kind of work he thought he did best.

Teddy did not hesitate a minute. "Political work," he said.

"Then," replied the editor, "you will become president of the United States."

Teddy did not brush aside the idea. He acted as if he'd already thought about it. If that should happen, he said, "I will do my part to make a good one."

But as the summer wore on, it was hard for westerners

to bank on optimistic talk. Hot and dry, the weather was against them. Cattle were going hungry, beef prices were falling, and unless the winter turned out to be a mild one, few of the cattle could be expected to survive. At the end of the summer Teddy's two Maine foremen were so discouraged that they gave up and went home. All Teddy could do was put his cattle in the care of the Maltese Cross Ranch and hope for the best. Of course he knew what people were saying about the wild creatures. They were preparing for a bad winter. Muskrats were growing extraheavy coats and beavers were storing away huge supplies. And the white Arctic owl had flown down from the far north. Only an emergency would bring that owl this far south.

In early October Teddy left the muskrats and beavers and headed for New York. If anyone had asked him how his cattle business was doing, he would have said, "Fine." After all, who knew what the Arctic owl's business really was?

Teddy and Edith's year of waiting was almost up, but before Teddy went to London, he wanted to attend the Republican county convention where a candidate for mayor of New York City would be nominated. Just because he was out of politics didn't mean he wasn't curious. And since this year three men would be running for mayor, it was bound to be interesting. The Labor Party had nominated a popular and powerful leader, Henry George, as its candidate, and now everyone wondered what the Republicans would do. Apparently the Republicans were wondering too, until they noticed Teddy Roosevelt in their midst. Why not Teddy? So one day a committee of Republicans called on Teddy, but when they asked him to become a candidate for mayor of New York City he didn't know what to say.

How could he not accept? The Republicans had asked him, hadn't they? And he was a loyal Republican. One who loved politics.

Yet how could he accept? With Henry George in the race, any Republican was apt to lose. But if he won, what would Edith say? He'd have to go to work on January 1, and that would be the end of the three-month honeymoon they had planned.

Teddy said yes, he would accept.

Obviously he couldn't resist the idea of getting into the race. So what if it was hard? He'd done hard things before. He'd lost before too. He wouldn't mind coming in second, he said. Just so he didn't come in third!

So he went to work—eighteen hours a day, three to five speeches a night, meeting after meeting. And because he was always cheered, he must have taken hope. Even a Democratic newspaper expressed its admiration for the way he was "working with all the strength of his blizzard-seasoned constitution. . . . He cannot be Mayor this year," the paper went on, "but who knows what may happen in some other year? Perhaps Congressman, Governor, Senator, President?"

Indeed, who knew? Oh, it was splendid to be back in the thick of things! Of course he wasn't tired. "Not in the least," he would say when anyone asked.

People loved Teddy Roosevelt for his youth, but many

wondered if a rambunctious twenty-eight-year-old should be trusted to run New York City. In the end, they decided no. The Democrat Abram Hewitt won; Henry George came in second; Roosevelt came in last. He tried to tell himself that at least his name was back in circulation, but that didn't make him feel better. So he put the election out of his mind, just as he did all unpleasant things, and on November 6 he and Bamie (who was in on the secret) boarded a ship for England.

On December 2, 1886, Theodore Roosevelt and Edith Carow were married in an eerie, almost invisible ceremony. London was so muffled in fog that except for the sounds, no one would have known a city was there. Teddy had to hire torchbearers to light the way for his carriage to get through the streets. Even inside, fog blanketed the church from top to bottom. Bamie said she couldn't see Teddy until she moved close, and perhaps even then she couldn't be sure it was Teddy until she looked at his hands. For some unexplained reason Teddy wore bright orange gloves to his wedding. In the midst of the clouds Teddy and Edith exchanged their vows.

In Europe on their honeymoon, Teddy wrote to Corinne how wonderful Edith was. He never referred to her as his "little wife." Edith was not that kind of person. She was a partner, and as rumors reached them about the severe winter in the West, she shared his worries about money. They even talked of selling Sagamore Hill and living on the ranch for a couple of years. They would simply have to wait and see.

4

A S IT TURNED out, those Arctic owls had known what they were doing. The winter of 1886–1887 was a killer. Snow lay over the prairies three to four feet deep, drifting as high as a hundred feet. A person did not dare to stay outside for too long for fear of being frozen to death, and of course the cattle had a rough time. Teddy didn't go West until April after the snows had melted, and although he'd heard all about the disasters, hearing was not the same as seeing. Riding the range, he came upon mounds of skeletons, cattle that had huddled together against the storms and been buried alive in the drifts. One carcass hung on a tree where the snow had left it. The few surviving cattle were no more than skin and bones, walking corpses. Even the land, brown and bare, looked as if it had been visited by death.

"I am bluer than indigo about the cattle," Teddy wrote Bamie. "It's even worse than I feared; I wish I was sure I would lose no more than half the money I invested out here."

In the end, Teddy sold out, losing $50,000 from his $85,000 investment. But at the time all he wanted was to get back East. Any idea of living on the ranch was gone, and rather than sell Sagamore Hill, Teddy and Edith decided simply to economize. They would sell part of the land and Teddy's hunting horse, raise chickens, grow their own vegetables, and cut down on the entertaining that Teddy loved to do.

And Teddy would write. Holed up at his desk in his third-floor gun room, Teddy finished a biography of Gouverneur Morris, prominent statesman in Revolutionary War days. Then he started on his biggest and most successful project, a four-volume history entitled *The Winning of the West.* He loved writing about the West, especially the battles, but it wasn't easy just to sit still describing heroic deeds and American heroes. He considered himself a "true American"—manly, red-blooded, honest, patriotic—and he wanted a chance to prove it. He was a doer, a talker, a persuader, a mover, and he longed above all to be close to the center of action. Since his early years when he had struggled against his body, he had found satisfaction in the very act of struggle. To be at his best, he needed to be fighting for something, and just as he had once wanted to improve himself, now he wanted to improve his country. "I would like . . . to go into politics," he admitted.

His chance came in 1889, when a Republican, Benjamin Harrison, became president and offered Teddy a job on the Civil Service Commission. He would be responsible for seeing that certain positions in the government (customs, postal services, for instance) were given out according to merit, not because of political or personal favoritism. He would have to make sure that there was no cheating on Civil Service examinations. Teddy's friends thought the job was beneath him, but not Teddy. He was dee-lighted. (The way he pounced down on the first syllable gave the word a joyfulness it didn't ordinarily have.) He sniffed corruption in the air. Good! Here was a chance to set things straight. So off he went to Washington, bounded up the steps of the Civil Service building, flung open the door to his office, and grinning his famous toothy grin, announced loudly that he had arrived.

Just as he expected, there was corruption. In Indianapolis, in Milwaukee, in Baltimore. Wherever he found it, he went after it, cracking down on wrongdoers, no matter how important they might be. Theodore Roosevelt made headlines and enemies, and he loved every minute. His only trouble, President Harrison said, was that he "wanted to put an end to all the evil in the world between sunrise and sunset." But why not? Teddy would have asked. In a jaunty straw hat, he whistled as he walked to work, but when he came to the White House, he would occasionally pause. "My heart would beat a little faster," he confessed much later, "as the thought came to me that possibly—*possibly*—I would some day occupy it as President."

So far, however, this was only a boy's dream. Every boy wanted to be president, he believed, but Teddy knew that he had "stirred things up" too much to expect any help up the political ladder. "Don't you know," he asked, "I have made an enemy of every professional politician in the United States? I can't have any political prospects."

And yet in 1895 he was asked again to run for mayor of New York. He was wild to accept but Edith said a firm no. They couldn't afford to pay for a campaign, and if Teddy lost, what then? Reluctantly Teddy gave up the idea, but he was so disappointed he couldn't settle down to his old job with any enthusiasm. Besides, after a little more than six years, he felt he had done what he could do. He was restless, bored, eager for a new challenge, but Grover Cleveland, a Democrat, was now in the White House. If Teddy didn't run for mayor, how could he hope for a change of job?

Of course he had diversions. At least once a year he went to Dakota country to hunt. He needed regular doses of western wildness even though the wildness was not what it once had been. He came back from a trip in 1887 reporting that trees were being cut down carelessly, animals were being slaughtered by "swinish game-butchers," and the wilderness was in danger. Obviously Teddy did not consider himself a "game-butcher." Even though he loved to hunt, it was on a small scale, a sportsman's pursuit, nothing that could endanger the environment, nothing like the wholesale killing that was going on and had been going on for years. Indians had killed herds of buffalo just for their tongues, which they sold as a delicacy.

Travelers shot buffalo out of train windows as target practice. People were chopping down trees and selling the lumber as if they expected the supply to last forever. Teddy knew this was happening, and as he rode through the Bad Lands, he was shocked at how quickly the region was being stripped of its glory. Not only was the big game gone, but beavers were disappearing, ponds were drying up, grass was giving way to desert.

As soon as he returned to the East, Roosevelt, desperate to save the West from extinction, founded the Boone & Crockett Club, dedicated to the preservation of wilderness in America. Largely through the club's influence, legislation was passed to take proper care of Yellowstone National Park, to protect sequoia trees in California, to set aside nature reserves for bird and sea life, and to limit the shooting of big game. The club also took steps to stop the "hounding of deer" (driving them into the water, where they would be easy to kill) and against blinding, or "jacklighting," game at night. For the rest of his life Theodore Roosevelt worked for conservation. He thought it sentimental to ban hunting altogether, so he continued to hunt; but conservation came first.

And Teddy had his family, an endless diversion. In late 1895 Teddy was thirty-seven years old and his family was almost complete. In addition to Alice, who was now eleven, there were young Ted Jr. (eight), Kermit (six), Ethel (four), and Archie (one). Quentin would arrive two years later. Ever the boy himself, Teddy created an ideal home for his children at Sagamore Hill, modeled in many respects on his own boyhood home. The children had their Pony Grant, just as he had once had. Christmas, the high point of his early years, followed the same pattern for his children as it had for him. Up at dawn, they would scramble on their parents' bed and open their stockings. Then together they would troop downstairs to the parlor, where a Christmas tree was waiting and where tables, one for each child, were piled high with their "big" presents. Christmas should be magic, Teddy believed; childhood should be magic, spilling over with animals, picnics, games, and laughter.

A friend once said of Teddy, "You must always remember that . . . [he] is about six." And indeed, among his own children Teddy abandoned himself to the joys of childhood. Down on all fours, he would play bear with the younger children, or "tickly." On the way upstairs he might be ambushed, and then he would either have to put up his hands or figure out a way to escape. On any summer day at Sagamore Hill a person might catch Teddy, together with his children, crawling through haystack tunnels in the barn following the leader. Or he might be up in a tree. Or out on the raft, where he'd be organizing a game of stagecoach. He would assign a position in a stagecoach to each child ("whip," "driver", "old lady passengers"), and then he'd tell a story. Whenever he mentioned a position, the child in that position would have to jump off the raft into the water. When he said "Stagecoach," everyone would have to jump off. The children considered Teddy their playmate but he was generally the leader.

It was this boyish spirit in him that people found hard

to resist, even though they might disagree with him. It was this same spirit that turned him into a dragon-slayer, determined to overcome all evil, as President Harrison said, "between sunrise and sunset." So perhaps it was not surprising that in the spring of 1895 the new reform-minded mayor of New York City should ask Teddy Roosevelt to be the city's police commissioner.

Everyone knew that the New York City Police Department needed to be cleaned up, and Teddy agreed that he was just the man to do it. Over the years he had learned that the first thing to do when he wanted to bring about reform was to get attention. He was an expert at this. Back in New York City, he went into high gear, made friends with two reporters whose office was directly across the street from his, and began a countdown on corruption. The police chief himself, Teddy discovered, had so many friends in the underworld that he overlooked whatever crimes he chose. In addition, all over the city, officers accepted bribes rather than enforce certain laws. Teddy went on a rampage, but whenever he was going to fire a high-ranking officer, he first stuck his head out of the window and let loose a loud cowboy "Hi-yi-yi" call. This was his signal to the reporters across the street that he was about to make news.

When Teddy said he would enforce the law, he really meant it. He would see to it that every patrolman paid strict attention to business on his nightly beat. Dressed in a long overcoat, his collar turned up, his hat pulled down, Teddy stalked the streets at night on the lookout for patrolmen who were neglecting their duty—slipping off for a nap or a drink or loafing on the corner with friends. Teddy would sometimes go forty hours without sleep, but what fun he had! Here he was, acting like a storybook character, stealthy, sly, pursuing evil in the dark of night. Patrolmen soon learned to look closely at any man in dark clothes with his hat pulled down. If he had a set of large white teeth, they knew they should look lively.

Teddy wore a bright pink shirt to work these days, and a black silk cummerbund with tassels reaching to his knees. As always, he was, as a friend said, "creating his own limelight," and indeed, he enjoyed the attention he was getting. It was only when he decided to enforce the law against selling liquor on Sunday that he ran into trouble. This was such an unpopular law that no one had bothered to enforce it. Teddy himself thought it was a foolish law but still it was a law, and he was determined to see that it was obeyed. But what a rumpus this made! Teddy got all of the publicity he'd ever wanted now. Papers throughout the country (and even one in London) wrote about him, most applauding him. But not those in New York City. Here everyone seemed to be against him, even members of his police board. He received two letter bombs in the mail, and a newspaper described him as "the most despised and at the same time best-loved man in the country," one who was bound to go higher. Mayor? the paper suggested. Governor? President?

All Teddy would admit after a year of his "grimy" job (as he called it now), after all the scrapping on the police board, was that he'd like to get into national politics. This was 1896, an election year, with William McKinley running for president on the Republican ticket. When he was asked to campaign for McKinley, he jumped at the chance. Grinning and waving and snapping out his words, he addressed one audience after another. He just hoped that McKinley noticed and that, if elected, McKinley would remember and appoint him to a position in government. Teddy didn't expect a cabinet post. What he really wanted was to be assistant secretary of the Navy.

Ever since Teddy had been at Harvard, writing about the Navy's part in the War of 1812, he had been fascinated by warships. He was convinced that if the United States had been properly prepared at sea, there wouldn't have been a War of 1812. He was also convinced that the Navy was still not prepared for war, and he believed that war was coming. At this time Cuba belonged to Spain and was ruled by a Spanish governor who dealt with protesting Cubans by shooting them—unarmed men and women alike—and sending them to prison camps. Teddy didn't like even the idea that Spain was in the Western Hemisphere, but if the nation wanted to free the Cubans and get Spain out, it would need a strong navy. Teddy was itching to get the Navy ready. He was also itching to get into a war if it came along. How would he ever know what war was like unless he fought in one? How would he know if he'd measure up?

When McKinley was elected, Teddy's friends went to him and urged him to give Teddy the post he wanted. But McKinley wasn't sure. He wanted peace, he said, and "Roosevelt is always in such a state of mind." He was too "pugnacious." It must have been hard for Teddy's friends to reassure the president that Teddy could be peaceful, but apparently they did. Teddy got the job.

When he arrived in Washington in April 1897, he told a reporter, "I am sedate now," and he almost convinced the president and his own boss, Secretary of the Navy John D. Long, that perhaps he had become sedate. He was charming, comparatively quiet, but all the while he was making friends with those in Washington who believed, as he did, that the United States should become a world power. It was not only Cuba that they wanted to set free: they wanted to annex the independent Hawaiian Islands, which were threatened, they believed, by Japan. Then there were the Philippine Islands in the Far East. They also belonged to Spain, so if Cuba were freed, the Philippines should be freed too. Teddy was on fire to start things moving, but for almost two months he kept quiet.

When he was asked to give a speech to the Naval War College in Newport, Rhode Island, on June 2, he could keep still no longer. Readiness was his theme. The only way to keep peace was to be ready for war, he insisted. The only way to be ready for war was to enlarge the Navy. He talked about "hard fighting virtues," he sneered at cowardice, and before he was through he had used the word "war" sixty-two times. It was a rousing, patriotic speech which delighted newspapers and inspired people generally to think of America in grander terms. Apparently it also encouraged some senators and President McKinley to do something about Hawaii. On June 16 the president approved a treaty to annex Hawaii and made it a territory of the United States. (The treaty wasn't ratified until a year later.)

Secretary of the Navy Long, however, was not pleased with Teddy's speech. He had gone too far with his private opinions, Long said; but then Long went on vacation and wasn't around to keep track of what went on. He wasn't there at the end of September, when Theodore Roosevelt presented the president with his own plan for freeing Cuba. (Within forty-eight hours after war was declared, fighting ships should leave Key West, Florida, for Cuba; they should be followed with a landing force. At the same time the fleet in the Pacific should blockade the Philippines, preventing Spanish ships from leaving, and possibly taking the capital, Manila.) Teddy hadn't finished. On the night before Long was due back in Washington, he intercepted a letter to Long, recommending that a certain Commodore William Chandler be appointed commander in chief of the Asiatic Station. Roosevelt was horrified at the idea of this timid man attacking Manila, and in a lightning move he got McKinley to write a note to Long, asking that Commodore George Dewey be given this post.

Again Long was unhappy, but what could you do with a man like Roosevelt? From this time events themselves dictated what was to come.

December 8, 1897. Commodore Dewey sailed for Hong Kong, to be within striking distance of the Philippines.

January 12, 1898. A riot broke out in Havana and Americans worried about the safety of their fellow citizens there. Not Secretary Long. He was impatient with the worriers and with Theodore Roosevelt. "He actually takes the thing seriously," Long wrote. "He bores me."

Teddy did take it seriously. He wrote to the head of the New York State National Guard, offering his services in case of war. (He would write again. "Remember . . . I want to go.")

January 25. The American battleship *Maine* dropped anchor in Havana harbor. This was a friendly visit, President McKinley explained. But it was also a warning.

February 15. The *Maine* was blown up. Two American officers and 264 sailors were killed. Did something go wrong on the ship to cause the explosion, or was it set from the outside by a submarine mine or torpedo? McKinley ordered an investigation, but Teddy Roosevelt said he had no doubt about what had happened. "It was an act of dirty treachery on the part of the Spaniards."

March. McKinley was still trying to avoid war at any cost and Spain showed signs of willingness to negotiate. But it was too late for the American people. Too late for Teddy Roosevelt, who told friends that McKinley had "no more backbone than a chocolate éclair."

March 28. The report on the investigation of the *Maine* disaster was published. Although now it is generally thought that the explosion was due to an accident on shipboard, at the time it was reported to have been caused by an "external device." That was all that Americans wanted to know. "Remember the *Maine!*" they cried from one end of the country to the other. It was a war cry.

April 11. President McKinley gave in to popular sentiment and asked Congress to declare war. On April 25 the formal declaration was made.

Three weeks later Teddy Roosevelt resigned as assistant secretary of the Navy so that he'd be ready to fight.

His friends told him he was crazy; he was throwing away his political future. Secretary Long said he was "acting like a fool." Edith was against it. She was recovering from a serious and expensive illness; young Ted had been sick; there was a five-month-old baby (Quentin) in the house. How could they manage without Teddy's salary?

Still, anyone who understood Teddy Roosevelt would know he had to go. He had spent his life fulfilling his boyhood dreams, and war (a *just* war, he would have said) was such a dream—the ultimate test of manliness, of patriotism, of bodily endurance. Even so, he felt he needed to explain himself. In case of a serious war, he wrote later, he wanted to be able to tell his children why he had fought in it, not why he hadn't fought in it. As his father had done, he might have added. This seemed to remain a sore point with Teddy all his life.

Again he said that he was the kind of person who couldn't preach one thing and do another. This was true. He was that kind of person.

On the other hand, he wrote a friend, "I say quite seriously that I shall nót go for my own pleasure. . . . I like life very much. . . . I have always led a joyous life. . . . So I shall not go into a war with any undue exhilaration of spirits."

This was only partly true. Teddy was exhilarated when he was given permission to raise a volunteer cavalry regiment. Because of his inexperience, he chose to be second in command, a lieutenant colonel, and gave first place to his good friend, an old Indian-fighter, Leonard Wood. Before going to Texas, where his regiment was to train,

Teddy ordered a light tan uniform trimmed in bright yellow, took out life insurance, and bought twelve pairs of steel-rimmed glasses, to be tucked away in every pocket of his uniform and even in his campaign hat. If he was going to fight in a war, he wanted to see what he was doing. Moreover, he wanted to be on time for it. He was terrified that somehow he would not be in on the first expedition. "It will be awful," he said, "if we miss the fun."

5

ALTHOUGH COLONEL Wood was recognized as being first in command, the public acted as if this were Teddy's regiment. At first, newspapers referred to the regiment as "Teddy's Terrors"; Roosevelt hated the nickname "Teddy," even though everyone except his family and close friends called him that. Soon the papers found the right name, the one that stuck. "Roosevelt's Rough Riders"—that's who they were, 1,000 men selected out of 20,000 applicants. The best riders, the best marksmen, the hardiest, they were a mixed lot—mostly cowboys from the Southwest, a few Native Americans, but also athletes from eastern colleges (a star football player from Harvard, a champion tennis player, high-jumpers from Yale). They wore blue kerchiefs around their necks, had a bald eagle for a mascot, sang "There'll Be a

Hot Time in the Old Town Tonight," and adored Lieutenant Colonel Roosevelt. They were men of a kind whose closeness turned out to be not just a wartime bond but a lifelong one.

Teddy was proud of them and was pleased with the way the war was going according to the plan he'd presented to the president. On May 1, Commodore Dewey had taken his fleet to the Philippines and in short order had destroyed almost every Spanish ship there. All without losing a single American life.

Now for Cuba. Of course it was important to have a quick victory in Cuba, but for Teddy it was absolutely essential that his regiment play a part in that victory. The question was: would their orders come in time? Would they be among the first to go?

He wrote to the president from Texas. "We are ready now to leave at any moment. And we earnestly hope that we will be put into Cuba with the very first troops; the sooner, the better."

At the end of May a telegram arrived, ordering the regiment to Tampa, Florida, "for immediate embarkation on transport ships."

It looked good. But immediate? Was anything in the Army really immediate? They didn't even leave immediately. After loading the horses on seven trains, the men found there were no trains for carrying them; they had to sleep beside the railroad tracks and wait until the next day to start.

It took four miserable, hot days to reach Tampa, and then, for some unexplained reason, the trains stopped seven miles short. So the Rough Riders mounted their horses and rode the rest of the way to the enormous tent city where the army was camped.

More waiting.

Three days later, on June 6, news came that despite their drilling on horseback, the Rough Riders were not going to operate as a cavalry regiment after all. Only the officers could take horses with them. Worse still, not all the men could go: only 560 out of the 1,000. Nothing that Teddy Roosevelt did in Cuba was harder than giving this news to those who couldn't go.

The next day the men were to leave, but the train that was to take them to the point of embarkation didn't appear. They were told to go to another track, but still no train came. And Teddy was not going to be left behind because of some foolish train mix-up. When he saw some coal cars, he told his men to climb aboard. So what if the engine was headed the wrong way? They simply told the engineer to go backward, and he did.

Finally they were at the water and could see the ships. They were told which ship they had been assigned to but two other regiments already had been assigned to the same ship. Still, the Rough Riders were *there,* and Teddy told them to get aboard on the double. Once they were on, he figured, no one would be able to get them off. Teddy simply told the other troops that he was under orders to hold the gangplank, and that's what his men did.

But did they sail? No. Some unidentified warships had been spotted at sea. The Rough Riders would have to wait until it was considered safe to go. Six days they waited, crowded in hot, stuffy quarters while horses died, food spoiled, and water turned bad. At last, on June 14, the regiments sailed—thirty-one transport ships stretched out over twenty-five miles of water—but they still weren't sure where they were going. No one had said they were going directly to Cuba; the official word was "destination unknown." Perhaps there was an intermediate spot where they would do some more waiting. Perhaps Puerto Rico. But no. When the fleet turned southwest, directly toward Cuba, a cheer went up from deck to deck of every ship. And Teddy Roosevelt, waving his hat in the air, broke into his Indian war dance.

Although the Rough Riders were expected to land after the men in the regular army had landed, Teddy, still afraid that he'd be left out of the fighting, managed to have his ship get to shore first. While the men splashed through the breakers to the beach, the horses were lowered into the water so they could swim. Teddy had two horses, but only one, Texas, made it. The other, Rain-in-the-Face, drowned. For several days the men were separated from their supplies; still, Roosevelt had his feet on Cuban soil, even though all he had with him were his gun, ammunition belt, sword, yellow raincoat, and a toothbrush. And of course twelve pairs of glasses.

Navy ships, which had preceded the transport ships, had bombarded the coastline and made it safe for the American troops to land. They had also blockaded the harbor at Santiago, a large seaport where Spanish ships were anchored. But in order to win this war, the city of Santiago had to be taken by land, and between Santiago and the American troops lay hills, heavily defended by the enemy. Time was on the side of the Spaniards. If the fighting went on too long, the Americans wouldn't have to be killed; they would die of malaria, yellow fever, and dysentery, jungle diseases that were new to them.

Along the shore they faced a difficult seven-mile stretch that had to be covered before the Army could turn inland. Refusing to ride while his men were on foot, Teddy marched with them in a downpour of rain. Then the Rough Riders, along with two regiments from the regular army, were ordered into the hills to attack the Spaniards in their advance positions. But who had ever seen country like this? A jungle of trees with branches twisting overhead, and underfoot the ground gone wild with growth. Insects swarmed, letting everyone know that they owned the place. Teddy Roosevelt's first impression of war was: It was confusing. "I had an awful time trying to get into the fight," he wrote later, "and trying to do what was right when in it and all the while I was thinking that I was the only man who did not know what I was about . . . whereas, as I found out later, pretty much everybody was as much in the dark as I was." To make matters worse, Teddy's sword kept getting between his legs as he walked. (He never wore it again.)

When the bullets came, they sounded, Teddy said, "like the ripping of a silk dress," followed sometimes by a pop which meant that someone had been hit. But where was the shooting coming from? In spite of all his glasses, Teddy couldn't see. Even when they came to a valley where the ground was more open, he still couldn't see, since the Spaniards were using smokeless gunpowder. Finally he did spot a trench with some cone-shaped hats sticking up from it. Once they had a visible target, the Rough Riders sent those cone-shaped hats running. Later they attacked a set of red-tiled ranch buildings from which the Spaniards were shooting, and again the Rough Riders were successful. They got rid of the Spanish soldiers and took possession of the buildings.

In this first experience with war, Teddy also had a chance to see its horrors. All the Rough Riders who survived would remember how their comrades were alive one minute, dead the next, and how almost immediately their bodies were attacked by giant land crabs clicking their claws and by vultures diving down for the kill. Teddy had expected horrors and he admitted that "war never changes its hideous phantasms." Still, over the years he had learned how to shut his mind to grief, so even when some of his best friends were shot, he would grit his teeth, knowing that his job was to take care of the living and go on with the war.

But at the end of this first day of skirmish, Teddy was still confused. What had really happened? Had they done well? Had he handled his troops correctly? When he met up with the three commanding generals and Colonel Wood, he wondered what they would say. As it turned out, he had done well and he was relieved to hear it. "As I was quite prepared to find I had committed some awful sin," he said, "I did my best to accept this in a nonchalant manner."

It was a week before the Americans made their big assault on San Juan Hill, their main target. In camp they washed their bloody uniforms, took care of their wounded, and scrounged for food since supplies had been so slow in coming. Teddy had already picked up three empty Spanish cartridges to take home as souvenirs for his children, and perhaps it was at this time that he wrote a letter to seven-year-old Ethel:

"Here there are lots of funny lizards that run about in the dusty roads very fast, and then stand with their heads up. Beautiful red cardinal birds and tanagers flit about in the woods, and the flowers are lovely. But you never saw such dust. . . . I have a mosquito net because there are so many mosquitoes."

The big battle for San Juan Hill took place on July 1, 1898, a day that Teddy would call "the great day of my life." No longer confused, he could feel his own power even before the fighting started. Two commanding generals had fallen ill with fever, so Colonel Wood was put in charge of one brigade, and as Teddy wrote, "to my intense delight, I got my regiment."

In battle, first in command of the Rough Riders, Colonel Roosevelt became a different man. Cool, calm, and very heroic, as one of his men reported, he acted deliberately, looked out for his men, and concentrated on his objective with an intensity that inspired confidence. This was real war today—massive, cruel, bloody, shattering. When the Rough Riders came to a creek, they found they had to wade through water already clogged with dead bodies and running with blood. Some didn't make it across the creek, but those who did fell into the tall grass on the other side and crawled forward on hands and knees so they would be hidden from the enemy. Not Teddy. Mounted on Texas, an easy target but somehow surviving, he rode up the lines of his men, keeping them straightened out and headed in the right direction.

Something primitive and animal-like in Teddy took over. There was no past, no future for him; there was only *now,* pitched at a height never experienced before. Teddy said he felt "the wolf rising" in him, and it was a wolf that would not be stopped. When he came to a contingent of Army regulars blocking his way, he asked why they didn't charge up and take the hill in front of them, which the Spaniards controlled. They couldn't do it, the officer in charge replied; they hadn't received orders. Teddy said he would give the orders, but still they didn't think this was enough. Perhaps they didn't want to think so. The Spaniards were on high ground with open country around them—a perfect military position for mowing down approaching troops. To Teddy it didn't matter how well positioned the Spaniards were. He was here to defeat them and he intended to do it.

"Then let my men through, sir," Teddy said.

"And I marched through," Teddy reported, "followed by my grinning men. . . . I waved my hat and went up the hill in a rush."

The Rough Riders took the hill. "Kettle Hill," they called it, because they had found a kettle at the top. It was not San Juan Hill but it was a hill that, no matter how difficult, had to be captured first.

San Juan Hill next. With Kettle Hill firmly in American

hands, the Rough Riders attacked San Juan Hill. They were the first to arrive and took part in capturing this important stronghold. When finally they could take a break, they cooked the food the fleeing Spaniards had left behind. Salted flying fish is what Teddy remembered, and they ate it, he said, "with relish."

Then the tired men of the regiment lay down on the hill for the night, knowing that although there would be more fighting, the worst was over. Eighty-nine of their men had been killed, the highest percentage of loss that any regiment had suffered, but Teddy believed that this only proved his regiment had been the bravest. In any case, he did not lie down with his men. He wasn't ready to rest. The wolf in him had not settled down. Here he was, the highest officer in command of the highest hill before Santiago and he knew now what battle was. He would never have to wonder again. He must also have suspected that with Americans on the edge of victory he might be considered a hero. One of his good friends, a reporter, was traveling with the Rough Riders, and when this reporter wrote stories, they made the headlines. Hour after hour, Colonel Theodore Roosevelt paced up and down San Juan Hill, glorying in his "great day" and in what he called his "crowded hour" at Kettle Hill. Later when he talked about that day (and he talked about it a great deal), he would wind up by saying, "It was a bully fight!" How he loved the word "bully"!

Two weeks and two days later, on July 17, the Spaniards officially surrendered, but it was a strange surrender. The Spanish general asked a favor of the

Americans. While the Spanish soldiers were handing over their weapons, would the Americans please bombard Santiago, aiming not *at* the buildings, but *over* them? That way, it would be less embarrassing for the general. He could say he had surrendered under fire. The Americans obliged him.

With the war over, the Rough Riders, and indeed all the American troops, were just as anxious to leave Cuba as they had been to get there. Every day more men were being struck down by malaria, but the War Department seemed in no hurry to bring them home. So in a formal letter written on August 3, Teddy Roosevelt pointed out "that his army must move at once, or perish." It was against all Army practice for an officer to address his superiors in Washington in this way, yet Teddy had the backing of many of the highest-ranking officers in Cuba.

The War Department was not pleased with the letter but it did act. And Teddy made the headlines again. Ever since his "great day" at San Juan Hill he had become America's hero, and there was talk of making him the new governor of New York. On August 15 a cheering crowd met the ship with the returning Rough Riders at Montauk Point on Long Island. Long before the ship could even dock, the crowd was calling for Teddy. He stood at the railing, a small figure waving his hat, but even from this distance his voice boomed out. "Oh, but we had a bully fight!" he shouted. He was "just like a boy," a newspaper reported, "who had thrown his lessons to the wind."

The crowd went wild. When Teddy arrived at Oyster Bay that evening, the people in the village rang every bell that could be rung and fired off anything that would make a noise. Teddy grinned his big grin and waved his hat furiously. There was no question about it: it was fun to be a hero, but he wasn't ready to talk about being governor. He hadn't finished being a colonel. After a short visit with his family, he went back to Montauk Point to be with "his boys" before they were mustered out of the Army.

On September 13 he finally had to say good-bye. It wasn't easy. As a surprise, the Rough Riders presented Teddy with a bronze statue of a broncobuster, waving his hat in typical Teddy fashion. Then they lined up before him to shake his hand. He said a personal good-bye, calling each one by name. Before it was over, many were in tears, and one private confessed that a handshake wasn't enough for a man like Teddy. He wished he could have hugged him. Still, it wasn't as final a good-bye as they all might have imagined. Those Rough Riders walked in and out of Teddy's life to the end of his days. One of the Riders was already looking to the future.

"Three cheers for the next governor of New York!" he shouted.

Four days later, on September 17, Theodore Roosevelt publicly announced that if nominated, he would agree to run for governor. Not everyone wanted him to go further in public life, however. Some were afraid of his big ideas and his superpatriotism. Did he want to turn the United States into an empire? they asked. But it was hard to put down a man as successful as Teddy. And he went on being successful. On the evening of September 25, he was informed that he had indeed been nominated as the Republican candidate.

Of course he made his usual vigorous campaign tour, a

whistle-stop trip through New York on a special train. He was accompanied by six Rough Riders in full uniform, one of them a bugler who blew the cavalry charge at every stop.

On November 8 he was elected governor of New York. He was in bed at Sagamore Hill when the news arrived. He put on his red dressing gown and went downstairs, and when he heard the news that he'd won by almost 18,000 votes, he grinned. "That's bully!" he said. But later, when he'd had time to reflect, he wondered about his future. He had just turned forty and momentarily he was a bit frightened. "I have played it in bull luck this summer," he said. "First to get into the war; then to get out of it; and then to get elected." Could such luck last? he asked a friend. He was at the crest. Would he begin to go downhill? "I may fail, you know," he admitted. Then suddenly he turned bashful. "It won't make any difference to you, will it?" he asked.

It was almost as if he were speaking to his father.

6

GOVERNOR ROOSEVELT, who was to be known as the "boy governor," understood that his success would depend a great deal on one man, United States Senator Thomas Platt of New York, the boss of the Republican Party's political machine. Teddy had tangled with Platt before, but he believed that if he were careful, he could get along with him, be independent, and be loyal to the party at the same time. He would "speak softly," he said, "and carry a big stick." (This would become one of Teddy's favorite expressions.)

When Teddy took office in Albany on January 2, 1899, he was obviously still a hero. More people turned out in subzero weather to cheer him than had ever been seen on the streets of the city before. The only reason the band didn't make more noise as it led the parade to the state capital was that the brass instruments had frozen in the cold. But nothing stopped the drummers. They thumped mightily as Teddy Roosevelt mounted the steps of the capitol, waving his high silk hat as if he were charging up Kettle Hill again.

When Teddy entered the Assembly chamber, he was greeted by a band, brass instruments and all, playing "Hail to the Chief." Then the members of both houses of the legislature broke into a college cheer:

"What's the matter with Teddy?
He's all right!"

Once Teddy got down to business, he made it clear that he might be all right, but he was still a reformer. One of the first things he did was to get rid of the uniformed honor guard that customarily accompanied the governor. He liked to walk fast and didn't want to be bothered by a batch of poker-faced military men, clicking their heels and snapping to attention. Besides, an honor guard cost the state money. Nor did Teddy think it was right for a governor to travel free on New York railroads. When he was sent a railroad pass, he returned it. "How I wish I wasn't a reformer," he wrote. "But I suppose I must live up to my part." No one minded such minor changes. And no one was surprised when he began holding twice-daily fifteen-minute news conferences with reporters. Teddy had always believed in publicity.

But Senator Platt did object when Governor Roosevelt turned down the man Platt wanted for superintendent of public works. Teddy spoke softly, but he was governor, he pointed out, and *he* made the appointments. When he tried appointing someone else, however, everyone he asked turned him down. Obviously Senator Platt was at work behind the scenes. What was Teddy to do? He had to prove that he was boss, yet he had to keep Platt happy. So he made a list of four men who would be acceptable to him and asked Platt to choose the man he wanted. This worked.

As governor, Teddy did bring about important reforms. Because he believed so strongly that all Americans should receive a fair chance, he made sure that working conditions for laborers were improved. He also wanted to put restraints on large corporations that he felt were profiting at the expense of the people. It was when he went after the corporations that he ran into trouble with Senator Platt. Specifically, Roosevelt was concerned about corporations that received their licenses from the state (for instance, transportation companies, and gas and electric companies) but were not required to turn any of their profits back to the state. They should be taxed, Roosevelt said. But Senator Platt had powerful friends in those corporations who contributed large sums of money to the Republican Party. Platt's followers did their best to block Roosevelt's tax legislation. They tried stalling, they tried amending the proposed bill, they told Roosevelt that his political future would be ruined if he went ahead with his plans. But Teddy did go ahead. He held out and he won. It was the major victory of his first year as governor, and Senator Platt was not pleased.

Teddy still had one more year to serve, but after that—what? Since his victory at San Juan Hill, more and more people were talking of Teddy as president. Of course he liked that. But he didn't want to run in 1900, the next presidential election year. McKinley would certainly try for a second term and he didn't want to oppose him. But 1904! That would be his year.

Teddy said nothing publicly about his hopes, but he did wonder what he should do until 1904. He wanted to run for another term as governor, even though he knew Senator Platt would probably oppose him. But if he were elected, that term would be over in 1902. Then what? Would the public still remember him in 1904? Would his luck last that long? In June 1899, one of Teddy's old friends suggested what he thought was a perfect solution. Since the current vice-president, Garret Hobart, was in poor health and would probably not seek another term, why shouldn't Teddy try for the vice-presidency on the McKinley ticket in 1900? That way he'd be in the public eye for four years and when McKinley's term was over, there he'd be, ready to run for the presidency. Edith didn't like this idea at all. She thought a vice-president had a worthless job. As for Teddy, he said he couldn't bear the thought of four years on the sidelines, watching other people make the news. "I should like a position with more work in it," he said.

Then on July 31, Vice-President Hobart announced that, healthy or not, he intended to run again for vice-president. So that was that.

But right now Roosevelt was still governor and he liked

the job. "Haven't we had fun being governor?" he wrote his sister Corinne. No matter what he was doing, he couldn't seem to help enjoying life. "On the whole," he once wrote, "I have continued all my life to have a better time year after year."

On November 21, 1899, Vice-President Hobart died. By this time, however, Teddy Roosevelt was too excited about his plans for new reforms in the state to give the vice-presidency much thought. He had big ideas for further controlling those corporations he had taxed, for adopting strict conservation measures, for replacing one of the officials he considered crooked. Senator Platt liked none of these suggestions. If Teddy Roosevelt was not taking the vice-presidency seriously, Platt was. Maneuvering Teddy onto the McKinley ticket, he decided, was the easiest way to get him out of New York politics and put an end to his everlasting reforms.

Teddy may not have realized it, but when he agreed to serve as a delegate-at-large to the Republican National Convention to be held in Philadelphia in June, he was in a way sealing his own fate. He kept insisting that he would not run for the vice-presidency. He said it over and over, but if he really had been determined not to run, he should not have gone to the convention. "Roosevelt might as well stand under Niagara Falls and try to spit water back," Platt said, "as to stop his nomination at this convention."

A Democratic opponent of Roosevelt's described to Edith what he thought would happen at the convention: "You will see a great number of the leading Republicans in the United States," he said. "And you will see nearly all of them at times acting like a lot of boys. When, for instance, some great leader comes into the Convention Hall, all will cheer and hundreds will jump up on their chairs, wave their hats, and shout their approval. And then—just a bit late—you will see your handsome husband come in and bedlam will at once break loose. . . . Then some two or three days later, you will see your husband unanimously nominated for the office of Vice President of the United States."

Edith interrupted. "You disagreeable thing," she complained. "I don't want to see him nominated for the vice-presidency."

The convention turned out to be much as the Democrat had predicted. Teddy, who knew how to make a dramatic entrance, did arrive "just a bit late" and attracted immediate attention with his wide-brimmed black felt hat, which could not be missed in the sea of flat-topped straw hats in the convention hall. And just as the friend had foreseen, the delegates went wild, jumping on their chairs. "We want Teddy! We want Teddy!" they chanted. Whenever he appeared, they took up the chant, some even following him to his hotel room.

Although Teddy Roosevelt still said no, it didn't sound like a positive no. Perhaps he found his own popularity hard to resist. Perhaps he wavered because of practical concerns. Senator Platt told him straight-out that he would support another candidate for governor of New York. Teddy accepted the challenge, but he must have recognized that perhaps he couldn't be governor again, even if he wanted to. Then what? He must also have been aware that there were a few powerful Republicans who didn't want him to be vice-president. Perhaps McKinley himself, although he didn't say so. But the chairman of the Republican Party, Mark Hanna, a close friend of McKinley, was violently opposed to Theodore Roosevelt. "Nothing but a damned cowboy," he said. When it became obvious that Roosevelt was going to get the nomination, Mark Hanna became desperate. "Don't you realize," he asked his friends, "that there is only one life between this madman and the presidency?"

In the end there was a stampede for Roosevelt, and as he accepted, banners waved, balloons fell, delegates cheered, and Edith Roosevelt, who was attending the convention, undoubtedly sighed. She did not want Teddy to be the vice-president and besides, she must have dreaded the coming months of the campaign. She knew that he would go racketing all over the country again, talking nonstop from the rear platforms of trains. And he did. Six hundred seventy-three speeches before election day. Twenty thousand words a day spoken to three million people in twenty-four states, but it must have helped. On November 6, President McKinley was elected to his second term and Theodore Roosevelt became the new vice-president.

His job would be presiding over meetings of the Senate. He was supposed to do this in a calm, neutral way without getting excited or giving opinions of his own. Some people wondered if Vice-President Roosevelt could even keep quiet that long, but no matter how he performed, this was hardly enough for a man who liked his days to be chock-full. He tried to comfort himself; at least he'd have more time at Sagamore Hill, more time to go hunting, more time to make speeches. But what else? Perhaps he would take up his law studies again. Perhaps he would give lectures on history at a college in or near Washington.

His term of office as governor of New York ended officially on January 1, 1901. After that he went to Colorado to hunt cougar, then back to Sagamore Hill on February 23; and a week later the whole family trooped to Washington for the inauguration on March 4. Congress met the next day but was in session for only four days before recessing, so Teddy didn't have much time to practice being calm and impartial. With the spring and summer to fill, he went hunting again, took a sailing expedition with his boys, visited Corinne at her summer home, went on a jaunt to Buffalo, New York, with Edith.

On September 4 he traveled to Vermont to deliver a few speeches; Edith, Kermit, and Ethel planned to join him afterward for a vacation in the Adirondacks. In the early evening of September 6, while Roosevelt was attending a large party at the home of a former governor of Vermont, he received a telephone call. Members of the household must have realized the gravity of the call, for while he was on the phone, all the doors of the house were locked and guards were placed at every door. President McKinley had been shot while visiting Buffalo. No one knew how serious the wound was, but everyone wondered: Was this a conspiracy? Would Theodore Roosevelt be the next target of an assassin's bullet?

Teddy left immediately for Buffalo. As it turned out, there was no conspiracy. McKinley had been shot by a demented man, an anarchist who was against the existence of any government. His right arm bandaged, he had approached McKinley in a reception line, and when the president had reached out to grasp the man's left hand, the man had shot him with a gun concealed in the bandage. The man was easily caught and fortunately McKinley did not seem to be fatally wounded. On September 10, doctors assured Teddy that the president was in good condition, recovering nicely, and Teddy could join his family, who were waiting for him at a clubhouse at the foot of Mount Marcy, the highest peak in the Adirondacks.

One of the first things he did on arriving at the clubhouse was to arrange for two ranger guides to accompany his party up the mountain. On Thursday, September 12, they began the climb—Teddy, Edith, Kermit, ten-year-old Ethel, a governess, three friends, and two rangers. That night they reached their overnight stop, two cabins located at an altitude of 3,500 feet. They had planned to continue the next day, but when they woke up, it was cold, drizzly, and so foggy they couldn't even see the top of the mountain. The women and children decided they'd had enough, so with one guide to lead them, they turned back down the mountain. Not Teddy. Whether he could see the top of the mountain or not, he knew it was there and if it was there, he had to get to it. So up he went with the other men in his party.

They reached the summit at about noon on Friday, September 13, and began the descent. At about one-thirty they came to a little lake called Tear-in-the-Clouds, which they decided was a good picnic spot. As he was eating, Teddy looked down the trail and saw a ranger approaching with a yellow telegram in his hand.

President McKinley had taken a turn for the worse and was not expected to live. Vice-President Roosevelt, who should have been in Buffalo immediately, had to walk ten miles to the bottom of the mountain, then find a wagon and a driver to take him the thirty-five miles to North Creek and the nearest railroad. It was night now and it must have seemed an endless one, for the wagon had to make its way through thick fog on a narrow trail that hung on the edge of cliffs. It was almost impossible to see, but if the driver hesitated, Teddy would tell him, "Go on; go right ahead." At dawn they finally reached North Creek where a special train was waiting for the vice-president. And there was another message. President McKinley was dead.

Teddy Roosevelt did not arrive in Buffalo until the afternoon. On the long train ride across New York State he was torn by emotions. He had wanted to be president, but not this way, oh! not this way. On the one hand, in spite of slighting remarks he had sometimes made about McKinley, he was genuinely fond of the man and saddened by his passing. On the other hand, he had wanted to make it to the presidency on his own, not get there, as he said, "through a dead man's shoes." Once he arrived in Buffalo, however, he was suddenly the president, although a mussed-up president dressed in traveling clothes. He borrowed an appropriate suit, and at 3:15 in the afternoon he took his oath of office in the presence of friends, many members of McKinley's cabinet, and a few reporters.

The next week was devoted to attending services and ceremonies in honor of President McKinley. Teddy wasn't ready to move into the White House until September 22, and since Edith was still at Sagamore Hill with the children, preparing for their move, he would be alone in Washington. He had determined that although he didn't like coming into the presidency in this way, he would not be morbid about it. Still, that first night in the White House would be an emotional time, and he invited his two sisters and their husbands to spend it with him.

As they sat at dinner, Teddy turned to Bamie and Corinne. "Do you realize," he asked, "that this is the birthday of our father, September twenty-second? I have realized it as I signed various papers all day long, and I feel that it is a good omen that I begin my duties in this house on this day. I feel as if my father's hand were on my shoulder, and as if there were a special blessing over the life I am to lead here."

7

TEDDY ROOSEVELT was forty-two years old when he became President, and his physical measurements (recorded the following year) showed how robust he had become: height, 5 feet, 8 inches; weight, 185 pounds; chest, 42 inches; collar, size 16½; hat, size 7½; shoes, size 9½. He was the youngest man to become president, and whether or not people worried about his youth, many did worry about his performance. Up to this time four vice-presidents had succeeded to the presidency on the death of the man in office. None had done well; all had been considered weak presidents. None had been reelected. No one, however, was worried about Theodore Roosevelt being a weak president. Indeed, someone once said that if Roosevelt ever became president, he'd give the country "national insomnia"; the worry was that he'd go swinging into office, upsetting the financial world, pushing ahead with his own ideas right and left. The country had, after all, voted for McKinley for president, not Roosevelt.

Teddy's brother-in-law (Corinne's husband) wrote to him. "I feel I must be frank," he said. "[If] when you start you will give the feeling that things are not to be changed and that you are going to be conservative, it will take weight off the public mind."

Mark Hanna, who had been favorably impressed with Teddy's behavior at the time of McKinley's death, advised him to "go slow." Teddy had already recognized the wisdom of such advice. When he took his oath, he announced that his aim was "to continue, absolutely unbroken, the policy of President McKinley for the peace, the prosperity, and the honor of our beloved country." He also asked all of McKinley's cabinet members to remain on his cabinet.

But Theodore Roosevelt was not William McKinley. The whole tone of the presidency changed with Teddy in charge, racing through days packed with business, bustling with visitors, astir with activity. Of course, as president he had to accept certain restrictions. He had to put up with Secret Service men at his side and he was warned to keep out of danger. At the beginning he tried. When he was given a new jumping horse, he promised to take him over very low fences, "as I have not the slightest intention," he said, "of risking an accident in my present position." For a while, because of McKinley's experience, he was asked not to shake hands in receiving lines, but this precaution didn't last long. On New Year's Day in 1907, he established a world record, shaking 8,150 hands in one day.

But Teddy was not going to let his presidency interfere with his family life any more than necessary. In the past the White House had been a decorous place, a gracious home, sometimes lonely, as it had often been in the years when Teddy's hero, Abraham Lincoln, had lived there. But now! No one had ever imagined the White House could be as boisterous as it became when the Roosevelts moved in.

Teddy described some of the pets that shared in the life of the White House. "There is Jack, the terrier, and Sailor Boy, the Chesapeake Bay dog; and Eli, the most gorgeous macaw . . . who crawls all over Ted, and whom I view with dark suspicion; and Jonathan, the piebald rat, of most friendly and affectionate nature, who also crawls all over everybody; and the flying squirrel, and two kangaroo rats; not to speak of Archie's pony, Algonquin." All of them seem to have had free run of the house, and once Algonquin was even sneaked into an elevator and taken upstairs to cheer up Archie when he was sick. From time to time more pets were added—the feisty kitten, Tom Quartz, for instance, who bit a well-known political leader in the ankle. And some were subtracted. When any died, the whole family joined in a funeral ceremony on the White House grounds.

Although he was busier than he'd ever been, Teddy Roosevelt worked in his office right in the White House, so he was in the midst of his family much of the time.

While he was signing papers and dictating letters, he might hear Archie and Quentin racing each other down the long hallways. Or clumping about on their stilts. If he looked out the window, he might see them in their sandbox, "hard at work arranging caverns or mountains, with runways for their marbles." Although the boys knew the rules about not interrupting their father at work, there were times when they simply couldn't wait to see him. When Quentin was loaned a king snake by the owner of an animal store he frequently visited, he was so excited he roller-skated pell-mell home, burst into his father's office, and dumped the three- to four-foot-long creature into his lap. As it happened, President Roosevelt was in conference with the attorney general, but he agreed that this was a grand snake before sending Quentin and the snake out of the room.

Roosevelt was generally tolerant about occasional interruptions and even some mischief-making, but he could become angry. One rainy day, for instance, Quentin had invited three friends to play with him. "They were very boisterous," the president reported in a letter to Archie, who was away at school. "Finally they made spit-balls and deliberately put them on the portraits [hanging on the walls]. I did not discover it until after dinner and then pulled Quentin out of bed and had him take them all off the portraits." He told Quentin that he could have no friends to see him and the other boys would not be allowed into the White House until the president decided they had been sufficiently punished. This story probably did not make it into the papers, for as eager as Teddy was to have the press cover political news, he did not like it poking into his private life. Quentin, who was obviously instructed not to give out such information, once replied to a reporter's question about his father: "Yes, I see him sometimes; but I know nothing of his family life."

Yet President Roosevelt led such an active life, it was impossible to keep it secret. Everyone knew that he played tennis as often as possible and that he wrestled with the middleweight champion of the District of Columbia. He also took lessons in jujitsu from a Mr. Yamashita. But perhaps he was best known for his walks. These were not sedate strolls but energetic obstacle hikes through Rock Creek Park with friends, visiting diplomats, anyone who was handy. He called these hikes "point to point" walks over courses he and his children had mapped out together. The object was to go straight from one point to another, following the leader, over or through or under all obstacles, but never around them. A companion on one of these walks described the obstacles: first, the sheer face of a rock where there was "about an inch and a half of space for the feet and a few small knobs for the hands to cling to," then up a chimney of rocks that could be scaled only by "alternate hunching of the shoulders and pushing of the elbows." After a series of such obstacles came Rock Creek itself. When the water was shallow enough for wading, Teddy stripped, carried his clothes over his head, and dressed on the other side. His companions did the same. But sometimes the water was deep, over one's head. Then "Roosevelt took out his watch," his friend reported, "put it in his hat and swam to the other

side with all his clothes on. . . . He ran along the bank to another deep place and swam back to the other side. We then walked about five miles to Washington, lying down occasionally on the sidewalk to let the water run out of our shoes."

Teddy knew that people had heard of his walks and perhaps were critical of them. "Do you think," he asked a friend, "that people object to my tramping through the park in top boots and a slouch hat?"

"You must not forget," the friend replied, "that you are the president and that you follow the most dignified man ever in the White House—William McKinley."

Roosevelt argued that when he was acting as president, he too was dignified.

"But Mr. President," the friend pointed out, "you are the president all the time."

He was also Theodore Roosevelt all the time. And he decided that he was not going to change his habits even if he was president.

When he could get away from Washington, Teddy Roosevelt still went hunting. He allowed no reporters on these trips, but stories leaked out and, whether true or not, his friends and enemies made the most of them. Mark Twain, for instance, who had never liked Roosevelt, made fun of a report (likely true) about Teddy hugging his guides after making a kill. "It is the President all over," Twain grumbled. "He is still fourteen years old. . . . He is always hugging something or somebody." On the other hand, when he was hunting bear in Mississippi and refused to kill an old bear, the newspapers got the story wrong and said it was a bear cub he had refused to kill. A cartoonist turned the story into a cartoon, and a toy company began manufacturing toy bear cubs, calling them "Teddybears." How much truth there was in the original story is not clear, but the Teddybears made a big hit and all over the country they began accompanying young children to bed. The president didn't mind having a stuffed toy named for him, but he did hate the nickname "Teddy." Why couldn't they have been called "Theodore bears"? he asked.

Although Theodore Roosevelt made room in his life for fun, he found that being president was a complicated business. He loved having "his hand on the lever," as he said; the trouble was that too many other people tried to put their hands there too. In exasperation, he often turned to Abraham Lincoln's letters for comfort. "I am more and more impressed every day not only with the man's wonderful power and sagacity, but with his literally endless patience, and at the same time his unflinching resolution." Roosevelt had no lack of resolution but his patience was not always endless. He knew exactly what needed to be done in the country, and although he tried, it was hard to "go slow."

Teddy recognized that in the last fifty years the United States had changed. It had become an industrial nation with worldwide interests; the government needed to adapt to new conditions and respond to new needs. When big business became too big, it needed to be curbed. If the workingman was imposed upon, he needed to be protected. In turn, if labor became too powerful, it would have to be restrained. The environment must be preserved. The United States should assert itself as a world power. In other words, Teddy Roosevelt believed that the government had to play a larger part in the life of the nation and the president had to play a larger part in the government. And the government had to give everyone what he called a "square deal."

Teddy didn't need to look for ways to put his ideas into action. One after another, emergencies arose where he could step in and assume leadership. When the great financier J. P. Morgan took control of all the northwestern railroad companies, President Roosevelt instructed his attorney general to file a suit. Since 1890 there had been a law (the Sherman Antitrust Act) that made it illegal for large corporations to acquire other companies across state lines. Since then the law had seldom been enforced, but Teddy intended to change that. He had to wait until 1904 to hear the result but in the end, the Supreme Court decided Teddy was right: Morgan had acted illegally. In the meantime, by clever maneuvering, he succeeded in getting Congress to create a Bureau of Corporations which would investigate the conduct of interstate corporations.

Almost at the same time he had a chance to take the side of the workingman. The anthracite coal miners of the United Mine Workers went on strike, demanding higher wages and better working conditions. But the operators of the mines refused even to talk to the miners. They were still refusing at the onset of winter when the country needed coal for heat. Teddy Roosevelt didn't care so much how the specific negotiations went, but he did want the mines reopened. The operators were behaving, he said, with "arrogant stupidity," and he decided it was time to bring out his big stick. He ordered federal troops to stand by, ready to go in and run the mines. There was a question whether a president had the constitutional right to do this, but as it turned out, Roosevelt didn't need to send the troops in. He was able to get both sides to accept the decision of an impartial board to referee the matter.

Perhaps the project dearest to Teddy's heart was the idea of joining the Atlantic and Pacific oceans by a canal across the fifty-mile-wide Isthmus of Panama. As a world power, the United States needed a quick route from one ocean to the other so it could establish its place on both sides of the world. A shortcut across the isthmus was not a new idea. In the sixteenth century the Spanish had seen the need and built a road. A private French company had only recently tried to build a canal but had gone bankrupt. In the 1850s a group of American businessmen had built a railroad across the isthmus. Teddy was a Navy man and he wanted a thruway for ships. In June 1902, after weeks of debate, Congress passed the Spooner Bill, authorizing the construction of an American canal in Panama.

But what about the people in Panama? Did they want a canal? They loved the idea but Panama was a colony of its neighbor, Colombia, which would have to make the decision. So in 1903 the United States worked out a treaty with the Colombian government, and when the United States Senate ratified the treaty, Teddy, like everyone else, thought it was settled. But the Colombian Senate refused to sign, claiming that the Americans were taking advantage of them. This is when Teddy Roosevelt's patience began to wear thin. In private letters to John Hay, his secretary of state, who was trying to negotiate the deal, Teddy referred to the Colombians as "contemptible little creatures," "jack rabbits," "inefficient bandits."

The people in Panama were also angry. *They* wanted the canal. Teddy let it be known that he would be "delighted if Panama were an independent state." Panamanians had come to the same conclusion, and on November 3, 1903, they began a revolution. It was short and successful, with one American gunboat anchored in the harbor, another on its way, and with the Panamanian railroad under orders from the United States not to transport Colombian troops. On November 6, Panama declared its independence and the United States recognized the Republic of Panama.

Perhaps nothing President Roosevelt did in office aroused as much criticism as this use of what some called "gunboat diplomacy." Teddy was accused of "land piracy," of stirring up a revolution, but he said he hadn't stirred up anything. He had simply "lifted his foot and let it happen." This was one way of putting it, but without those gunboats and without American cooperation, it is doubtful that Panama would have won its independence as easily. Americans who had always been uneasy about Teddy's hand being "on the lever" became even more uneasy. What would he do next? Mark Twain was one of those who worried. "I think he longs for a big war," he said. But as far as Teddy was concerned, he had just cut through red tape so he could get the canal started. And indeed, within six months it was started.

Running beneath all Teddy's other interests in this term of office, however, was his overwhelming ambition to be elected to the presidency in 1904. Now he was simply president in the place of McKinley. "An accidental president," he called himself. He wanted to be president in his own right. "I'd rather be elected to that office," he said, "than have anything . . . I know. But I shall never be elected. *They* don't want it." He meant that the Republican bosses—Mark Hanna, Senator Platt, and the rest— didn't want it. They sided with men from big business in forming a strong conservative force in the Republican Party, fighting for the right to be free and make as much money as they could, whether it harmed people or not. So as the election approached, Teddy did his best to win these men over, reassuring them, consulting with them, even inviting J. P. Morgan to the White House. But Teddy need not have worried. He was more popular with the American public than he supposed. At the Republican National Convention in June 1904, he was unanimously chosen as the presidential candidate. On November 8 he was elected president in his own right by a greater popular majority than any recorded up to that time.

Theodore Roosevelt's inauguration day, March 4, 1905, must have ranked, along with his day at San Juan Hill, as one of the happiest of his life. On the night before the inauguration, Secretary of State John Hay, who had once been Abraham Lincoln's private secretary, gave him a ring containing a lock of Lincoln's hair. "Please wear it tomorrow," Hay wrote. "You are one of the men who most thoroughly understands and appreciates Lincoln." With this ring on his finger, Theodore Roosevelt took his oath of office on the porch of the Capitol, his shoulders back, his voice ringing out against a strong wind as if he were directing his promise to every man, woman, and child in the country as well as to the powers above. Teddy threw himself whole-heartedly into the inaugural festivities. In the afternoon he took his place in the front box of the reviewing stand, saluting and cheering as the grand parade marched by—governors, Army and Navy cadets, state organizations, Native Americans, Harvard men, and more. There was one group Teddy was particularly eager to see: the Rough Riders. They had served as his honor guard at the inauguration ceremony, and when they came down the road they were riding at full gallop, swirling their lassos, waving their hats. A band played "There'll Be a Hot Time in the Old Town Tonight," and for a few moments President Roosevelt became Colonel Roosevelt again, his face aglow, his body swaying, his arms swinging in time to the music.

Teddy was forty-six years old. He had gained forty pounds during his first term in office (he weighed 225 pounds now) which showed that he had kept busy not only at his desk and on the tennis courts but at the dinner table as well. Now as he went back to work, he tried to extend his reforms and proposed new ones, including a few that were rather strange. Once, in a burst of morality, Teddy, a firm believer in family life, suggested that marriage and divorce should be regulated by the federal government, perhaps even by an amendment to the Constitution. On another occasion he introduced the idea of adopting a simplified spelling system. About three hundred words would be changed—"thru" for "through," for instance, "thoroly" for "thoroughly," "dropt" for "dropped." These ideas didn't get far. Nor did his suggestion that the motto "In God We Trust" be dropped from coins. He thought it was blasphemous to put "God" on money.

Sometimes it was hard to tell what Teddy would do next. But in August 1905, he must have surprised Mark Twain and others who accused him of having a warlike disposition. At the moment a war was being waged in the Far East; but Teddy didn't try to enter it, nor did he support it. Instead he stopped it. For more than a year Russia had been fighting Japan in Manchuria, and Roosevelt did not think it was in America's interest for either of these nations to become too strong in the Pacific. So in the hope of helping the countries reach a settlement, he invited their representatives to come to Portsmouth, New Hampshire, for a peace conference. When they all came together, Teddy found that making peace was almost harder than making war. He had to be polite and sympathetic and patient with both the Japanese and the Russians, he said, when all the time he wanted to "jump up and knock their heads together." His patience paid off, however; a compromise was reached and a peace treaty was signed on September 5, 1905. In appreciation for his services in giving peace to the world, President Roosevelt was awarded the Nobel Prize for Peace.

Two years later, in another grand show of peace, Teddy had the American fleet painted white and sent it around the world on a tour of friendship. This would show the world, he figured, not only how peaceful America was but how strong it was. Some Americans predicted that this display of power would bring on war, but as it turned out, the tour was a success and Roosevelt was again hailed as a peacemaker.

In addition, Teddy Roosevelt continued to work, as he always had, for conservation. As a leader of the Boone & Crockett Club, he had worked to save forests and wildlife. As governor of New York, he had come out against the polluting of Adirondack streams and had pushed for laws to protect birds, especially songbirds, from being destroyed just so hatmakers would have pretty feathers to decorate ladies' hats. When he finally became president in his own right, he said, "Watch out for me!" He had many kinds of changes in mind for America, but nothing was more important to him than to change the way Americans used their land and their natural resources. Unless they began to think more of the public good and less of private gain, there would be little left for future generations to enjoy. At every opportunity, he tried to educate the public to the dangers of waste and pollution, and it is no wonder that he became known as the "Conservation President." During his time in the White House he established 150 national forests, the first fifty-five bird and game preserves, and five national parks. Under the National Monuments Act he set aside the first eighteen "national monuments," including Devil's Tower in Wyoming, the Grand Canyon, California's Muir Woods, Arizona's Petrified Forest, and Washington's Mount Olympus. Indeed, Theodore Roosevelt deserves much of the credit for teaching Americans to respect what nature has given them. When the National Wildlife Federation established a Conservation Hall of Fame in 1965, Theodore Roosevelt was given first place. John Muir came in second, John James Audubon fifth, and Henry David Thoreau sixth.

If Roosevelt was praised for some of his actions, he was, like all presidents, blamed for things he couldn't help. When the country ran into hard times and people lost money, he was blamed. George Washington had the same problem, a friend pointed out. He complained that he was held responsible even for the weather. Teddy didn't complain but his face showed the strain of his years in office. Still, being president was fun, he insisted. "No president," he said, "has ever enjoyed himself as much as I have enjoyed myself."

But it would soon be over. At the time of his election he had stated publicly that he would not run for another term. Like George Washington, he did not believe it was wise to have the same man as president three times at a stretch. Yet here he was, not quite fifty years old, passing the crest of his career, and already he had fulfilled all his boyhood dreams. Ready or not, he had to take his hand off the lever.

It was hard for Teddy to let go. And it was hard for Americans to let him go. At the Republican National Convention in 1908 such a wild clamor broke out for Teddy that it almost seemed the people would make him president again whether he agreed or not. Delegates and visitors alike stood on chairs, shouted, waved Teddybears, took off their coats and swung them around their heads. For fifty minutes they kept this up, and no matter how hard the chairman rapped for order, it made no difference. When the time came for nominations to be made, Teddy Roosevelt had to telephone the convention from the White House, stating again that he would not be a candidate.

Whether people agreed with all Roosevelt's policies or not, most could not help loving him. There was such warmth to the man, such life, that even people who didn't know him felt he was their friend. Farmers living near railroad tracks would light up their houses when they heard that Teddy would be riding by. In the middle of the night they would step out on their porches and wave at the train. They knew that Teddy wouldn't see them but they wanted to salute him anyway.

Everyone recognized that Theodore Roosevelt was like no one else. A visiting Englishman put it this way: America had two natural wonders—Niagara Falls and Theodore Roosevelt. A Chicago newspaperman wrote an article in praise of Teddy, addressing him directly:

Ah the fun of you and the glory of you! Where lies the American whose passion or whose imagination you have not set a-tingling? . . . Before you came, all in politics was set and regular. Those who were ordained to rule over us did so with that gravity with which stupid grown-ups so oft repress the child. No one ever talked to us as you did. . . . They never took us by the hand and laughed and played with us as you did.

And then you came!

Dancing down the road—you came with life and love and courage and fun stickin' out all over you. How we loved you at first sight! And how you loved us!

Teddy's final days at the White House were busy with farewells as well as preparations for his next step. Of course he wanted his policies to be carried forward in the next administration, so he had handpicked the Republican he hoped would win the election. His good friend William Howard Taft was his choice, and to Teddy's great satisfaction he was elected. Now it was a matter of good-byes. Teddy gave a number of White House dinners for dignitaries and friends, and in turn he was flooded with farewell letters. Between fifteen and twenty thousand arrived in his last week alone.

What now?

Teddy had no intention of retiring full-time to his rocking chair. Adventure—that's what he wanted. He and Kermit (under the sponsorship of the Smithsonian Institution in Washington, D.C.) were going to Africa to hunt—lion, rhinoceros, hippopotamus, anything Africa offered. Corinne asked her brother what kind of present she could give him for the trip. Teddy didn't hesitate. "A pigskin library," he said. Theodore Roosevelt couldn't go anywhere without a supply of books to read. But in Africa ordinary book bindings would fall apart, so he asked Corinne to have the books specially bound in pigskin. He gave her a list of sixty books, which she had bound and which indeed accompanied him on the back of burros through the jungles.

Taft was duly inaugurated as president and Teddy set sail, waving to the vast crowd that had come to see him off, waving and waving until the United States gradually faded from sight. Then it was: Hurrah! Full steam ahead for the lions.

Afterword

THEODORE ROOSEVELT stayed abroad for a year. On his return he was distressed to find that President Taft, falling into the grip of conservative Republicans, had not followed Roosevelt's ideas at all. So Teddy began speaking out in public for those policies he had always upheld. Still popular, he soon had a following, and at the Republican National Convention in 1912, many delegates supported him for the presidential nomination. The convention, however, was controlled by Taft people, who found a technical way of refusing to allow many of the Roosevelt delegates to vote. As a result, Roosevelt's supporters walked out, formed a third party, the Progressive Party (nicknamed the "Bull Moose Party," after Teddy), and ran him at the head of their ticket.

Teddy was not ambitious to be president again, but he

was furious at the injustice that had kept him from making a fair fight at the convention. Although he knew he had no chance of winning, he was in a frenzy of righteousness, convinced he had "to give the right trend to democracy—away from shortsighted, greedy materialism." As predicted, the Democratic candidate, Woodrow Wilson, won the election; Roosevelt came in second, and Taft third. Some of Teddy's best friends felt his reentry into politics had been a mistake. In any case, he did not prolong the life of the Progressive Party and for the next presidential election he rejoined the Republicans.

In the meantime he went on an expedition to Brazil in search of the source of a mystery river known as the River of Doubt. This was his last chance to be a boy, he said, but it turned out to be a nightmarish test of endurance in a land of fever, mosquitoes, swarms of bees, fighting flies, and biting ants that not only attacked people but also ate their clothes. Teddy, with an infected leg and high fever, came out alive but barely so. The expedition did accomplish its mission, however, and the Brazilians renamed the mystery river Rio Teodoro, in honor of Teddy.

Back in the United States, everyone was talking about the big war which had started in Europe. Teddy talked too. Although the United States was not in the war, it should be preparing for war, Teddy insisted, in case it was drawn in. In 1917 the United States did enter the war, and Teddy could hardly wait to join up. He offered to raise a volunteer division but Woodrow Wilson said he was too old. To stay on the sidelines of a world war was hard for Teddy to take, but he had no choice. His one consolation was that all four of his sons served overseas.

Quentin was a pilot in the Army Air Corps; on July 14, 1918, he was shot down and killed. "I feel as though I were a hundred years old," Teddy said, "and had never been young."

Six months later, on January 6, 1919, Teddy, who had not been strong since his Brazilian trip, died in his sleep from a blood clot in his heart. He was sixty years old and had done what he had promised himself he would do. He had lived full-tilt, and as one friend reported, "he died with his spurs on."

Archie sent a telegram to his brothers, who were still in Europe. Like everyone else, Archie had to reach for a word that was bigger than man size.

"The old lion is dead," he wired.

Notes

Smithsonian Institution in Washington, D.C., and some to the American Museum of Natural History in New York City.

37   The head still hangs in the North Room at Sagamore Hill.

40   Alice had Bright's disease, which attacks the kidneys.

56   In 1894, while Teddy was with the Civil Service Commission, his brother died, an alcoholic. Elliott's problem was long-standing, and although Teddy tried to help, Elliott would not let himself be helped. Corinne said she had never seen Teddy cry as he did when Elliott died.

67   Ted had a mild nervous breakdown, due, it was thought, to his worrying about living up to his father's expectations. Theodore Roosevelt didn't realize he was pushing his son so hard, and he regretted it.

72   A naval launch, commanded by a friend of Teddy's, came alongside Teddy's ship and helped with the landing.

75   This letter to Ethel, dated May 20, was obviously misdated, since the Americans weren't even in Cuba in May.

80   Teddy wanted very much to be awarded the Congressional Medal of Honor and indeed expected it. He was to be disappointed. Probably his letter to the War Department had angered the administration.

80   The statue was made by the famous artist Frederic Remington.

90   The Pan-American Exposition was being held in Buffalo and was attracting many visitors.

94   Edith had stayed behind with the children and so was not present.

99   When the boys were considered old enough, they went to

prep school at Groton, in Connecticut. Later they went to college at Harvard.

105   J. P. Morgan arranged for the incorporation of the Northern Securities Company, which was created to take over railroads in the Northwest until it had a monopoly.

107   In November 1906, Roosevelt made a quick trip to Panama to check on the progress of the canal. It was not actually completed until 1914.

117   A fish and an elk were also named for Roosevelt. A Hawaiian fish (yellow with black bands) was given the name *Roosevelti.* A new species of elk found in Oregon was called *Cervus roosevelti.* Later it was downgraded to a subspecies but Roosevelt was still remembered in the name: *Cervus canadensis roosevelti.*

Bibliography

Abbott, Lawrence. *Impressions of Theodore Roosevelt.* Garden City: Doubleday, 1919.

Boller, Paul F., Jr. *Presidential Anecdotes.* New York: Oxford University Press, 1981.

Brooks, Chester L., and Ray H. Mattison. *Theodore Roosevelt and the Dakota Badlands.* Washington, D.C.: National Park Service, 1958.

Chessman, G. Wallace. *Theodore Roosevelt and the Politics of Power.* Boston: Little, Brown, 1969.

Cutright, Paul Russell. *Theodore Roosevelt: The Making of a Conservationist.* Urbana and Chicago: University of Illinois Press, 1985.

DeVoto, Bernard. *Mark Twain in Eruption.* New York: Capricorn Books, 1968.

Hagedorn, Hermann. *The Roosevelt Family of Sagamore Hill.* New York: Macmillan, 1954.

Harbaugh, William Henry. *Power and Responsibility: The Life and*

Times of Theodore Roosevelt. New York: Farrar, Straus and Cudahy, 1961.

Lewis, William Draper. *The Life of Theodore Roosevelt*. Chicago and Philadelphia: John C. Winston, 1919.

McCullough, David. *Mornings on Horseback*. New York: Simon & Schuster, 1981.

Morison, Elting E., ed. *The Letters of Theodore Roosevelt*. Cambridge, Massachusetts: Harvard University Press, 1951–1954.

Morris, Edmund. *The Rise of Theodore Roosevelt*. New York: Coward, McCann & Geoghegan, 1979.

Pringle, Henry. *Theodore Roosevelt: A Biography*. New York: Harcourt, Brace, 1931.

Putnam, Carleton. *Theodore Roosevelt: The Formative Years 1858–1886*. New York: Charles Scribner's Sons, 1958.

Robinson, Corinne Roosevelt. *My Brother Theodore Roosevelt*. New York: Charles Scribner's Sons, 1921.

Roosevelt, Theodore. *An Autobiography*. New York: Charles Scribner's Sons, 1920.

———. *Diaries of Boyhood and Youth*. New York: Charles Scribner's Sons, 1928.

———. *The Free Citizen*, ed. Hermann Hagedorn. New York: Macmillan, 1956.

———. *Theodore Roosevelt's Letters to His Children*. New York: Charles Scribner's Sons, 1928.

———. *Works*, ed. Hermann Hagedorn (National Edition, 20 vols.). New York: Charles Scribner's Sons, 1926.

St. George, Judith. *Panama Canal: Gateway to the World*. New York: G. P. Putnam's Sons, 1989.

Wister, Owen. *Roosevelt: The Story of a Friendship*. New York: Macmillan, 1930.

Wood, Frederick S. *Roosevelt As We Knew Him*. Chicago and Philadelphia: John C. Winston, 1927.

Index

as police commissioner of
New York City, 61–62
politics, early interest in,
27–29
as president of the United
States, 94–100, 103–15
Progressive (Bull Moose)
Party and, 116–17
Rough Riders and, 69–76,
79–82, 108, 109
Sagamore Hill and, 45, 49, 52,
54, 59–60, 82, 90, 95
San Juan Hill and, 74–76, 79,
80, 108
Spanish-American War and,
64–76, 79–81, 108
"square deal" of, 105
*Summer Birds of the
Adirondacks, The,* 23
"Teddybears" and, 103–4, 113
United Mine Workers strike
and, 105–6
as vice president of the United
States, 86–90, 93–94
War of 1812 and, 25, 27, 29,
63
the West and, 34–37, 41–46,
49–50, 52–54, 56, 59, 90
Winning of the West, The, 54
World War I and, 117–18
as a writer, 23, 25, 27, 43, 49,
54, 63
young adulthood of, 19–26
Roosevelt, Theodore, Sr. (father),
38
death of, 23, 24
influence of, on Teddy, 10–12,
15–16, 19, 20, 23, 27, 30,
40, 44, 67, 95
Rough Riders, 69–73, 81–82,
109
at San Juan Hill, 74–76, 79, 80,
108

–S–
Sagamore Hill, 45, 49, 52, 54,
59–60, 82, 90, 95
San Juan Hill, 74–76, 79, 80, 108
Sherman Antitrust Act, 105
Smithsonian Institution, 114
Spanish-American War, 64–65,
81
Maine, U.S.S., 66
San Juan Hill, 74–76, 79, 80,
108
Spooner Bill, 106
"Square deal," 105
*Summer Birds of the
Adirondacks, The*
(Roosevelt), 23
Supreme Court, 105

–T–
Taft, William Howard, 114–17
"Teddybears," 113
origin of, 103–4
Thoreau, Henry David, 112
Twain, Mark, 9, 103, 107–8, 110

–U–
United Mine Workers strike,
105–6

–W–
War of 1812, 25, 27, 29, 63
Washington, George, 112
Wilson, Woodrow, 117
Winning of the West, The
(Roosevelt), 54
Wood, Leonard, 67, 69, 74, 75
World War I, 117–18

–Y–
Yamashita, Mr., 100
Yellowstone National Park, 59